PETER'S TREASURE

A PETER PAN RETELLING

KAYLEE JOHNSTON

For Russell - the love of my life

Happy Anniversary

1

"Get a move on, you scally-wags! We need to set sail in order to capture the treasure. Or do you not want to partake in the mighty riches that await us?" Peter's commanding voice shook through the rails of the ship, causing all of the boys to stop and snap their eyes toward him.

"No sir!" They all cried, scrambling to get back to their posts. Peter's eye was drawn to one scrawny boy with brown hair that fell over his eyes. He sighed as he watched the boy trip several times as he ran to get to his post. Peter closed his eyes as the boy stepped into a bucket full of soapy water, tripped, and threw the bucket over half of the ship, causing a few other boys to trip and fall.

"Tootles, bring me Too Small. He's causing trouble again," Peter directed his first mate, who was standing behind him. Peter turned, not bothering to watch his crew finish getting ready to set sail. He trusted them to do what needed to be done or face the consequences. He walked down the staircase and turned to the doors that were under the helm. He threw open the double doors to his cabin.

He sighed as he took in his surroundings. The large cabin was furnished with ornate, but mismatched furniture. A dark oak chest sat in one corner. A large mahogany bed sat under the rear windows. A spruce colored dresser sat under a pile of shirts discarded on top. A deep burgundy armchair sat on the other side of the room. In the middle of it, a maple desk commanded the attention of the room. All of these, spoils of the last few times they had bested Captain Hook and his men.

Peter's favorite was the grandfather clock that stood near his bed. It overlooked where he slept, giving off a peaceful tick tock as he dreamed of the crocodile finishing off Captain Hook. Peter walked into the cabin, settling into his desk. He was not looking forward to this conversation. Tootles walked in with Too Small limping close behind him.

"Captain? Too Small here to see you," Tootles said, clearing his throat.

"Yes, yes, thank you. You're dismissed," Peter responded, waving Tootles off. Tootles shut the double doors as he left the room. Too Small let out a terrified squeak.

"Too Small?" Peter asked. Too Small's eyes had grown wide and Peter noted he was covered in sweat.

"Do you know what the key objective is on a ship, Too Small?" Peter asked. Too Small shook his head.

"It's to work like a well-oiled, finely tuned machine. Every person on the ship must have some type of job and duty to keep this ship afloat. Every person needs to work together in order to make sure things are ship-shaped around here. A ship is only as strong as its weakest crew member. Who do you think our weakest crew member is, Too Small?" Peter asked, raising an eyebrow.

"Me?" Too Small squeaked. Peter took a deep breath and nodded.

"Do I have to walk the plank now?" Too Small asked. Peter considered it for a minute but thought of something else.

"Too Small, do you know anything about the treasure we're going after?" Peter asked, standing up and going to stare out the side window. He felt Too Small hesitate.

"Which treasure is that, Peter?" Too Small asked. Peter turned around.

"Pirate treasure," Peter replied, his eyes gleaming with excitement. Too Small gulped. It was never a good thing when Peter had that look in his eye. It meant they were going to do something dangerous and reckless.

"No, Peter. I can't say that I do," Too Small squeaked. He hoped that his lack of knowledge would disappoint Peter and cause him to drop the idea. Peter would do no such thing. After coming up with an idea that excited him, Peter would do anything to make it happen. It didn't matter the risks. All that mattered was the adventure.

"We're going after Captain Hook's treasure," Peter said, his voice rising with eagerness. Too Small gulped again.

"How do you know where it is, Peter? How are we going to get it? Captain Hook is the most dastardly evil pirate across the seas. He will surely be the end of us," Too Small pleaded. Peter narrowed his eyes and a crooked smirk slid onto his face.

"Nay! Captain Hook is the greatest adventure on these seas. The map is on Skull Rock and his treasure is on the Jolly Roger island, of course!" Peter exclaimed. Too Small gasped.

"But Peter, Captain Hook is looking for us ever since you cut off his hand and fed it to that crocodile. He wants to kill us!" Too Small cried in despair.

"I know. Won't it be an awfully big adventure?" Peter smiled. Too Small shook his head in defeat.

"If you wish, Peter. What would you like me to do?" Too Small asked. Peter put his arm around Too Small's shoulders and steered him toward the double doors of his cabin.

"You have a very important job, Too Small. You are going to listen to the crew and tell me if any of them say anything negative about my brilliant plan. Do you understand?" Peter instructed. Too Small looked worried, but he didn't want to argue with Peter. He nodded. Peter's face erupted in a huge smile. He opened the doors and guided Too Small out of the cabin. He left Too Small and walked up the steps toward the helm of the ship. The crew was working in fine order.

"Captain," Tootles commented.

"Tootles, this is going to be my grandest adventure yet. Wait until we tell the lads," Peter smiled to himself.

"Sounds frightfully amazing," Tootles agreed.

"Gather the boys' attention, Tootles," Peter commanded.

"Aye sir," Tootles said, stepping forward.

"Avast ye, hearties! Captain has some wonderful news," Tootles called out. The entire crew stopped what they were doing and turned to look at Peter. Peter broke out into a brilliant smile. He couldn't wait to tell them his plan.

"We're going to steal Captain Hook's treasure!" Peter exclaimed, throwing his hands up in the air. None of the boys cheered. In fact, they all remained silent, glancing at each other with worried and confused looks.

"Captain?" Nibs, the bravest of the crew, stepped forward. Peter put his arms down and turned to look at him.

"Yes, Nibs?" Peter said, still wearing a smile. Nibs shifted, unnerved by Peter's reaction.

"We're going after Captain Hook's treasure, sir?" Nibs asked.

"I believe that is what I said. Is it not what I said, Tootles?" Peter turned to look at Tootles.

"Aye, sir. It is what you said." Tootles confirmed. Peter turned back to Nibs.

"Any other questions, Nibs?" Peter asked. Nibs glanced at the other lost boys. He wrung his hands nervously. He looked back at Peter, fear plain in his eyes.

"Aye, Captain, one more. How would we go about getting Captain Hook's treasure?" Nibs asked, his voice squeaking at the end. Peter grinned from ear to ear.

"By having an awfully wonderful adventure," Peter responded. Nibs gulped and nodded. Tootles stepped forward.

"Back to your stations, lads! Hop to it!" The lost boys scrambled to get back to their stations and get the ship moving again.

"Peter, we are underway again," Tootles said, coming to stand at the helm. Peter nodded, excitement buzzing through his body. Tootles left the wheel and came to stand next to Peter, overlooking the frenzy of activity happening below.

"Peter, there's something I need to say," Tootles said, his voice shaking ever so slightly. Peter turned to him, frowning.

"What is it?" Peter asked. Tootles swallowed, not sure how to say what he needed to without upsetting Peter. He took a deep breath.

"I think we need to go over what you plan to do some more," Tootles said slowly. Peter's frown deepened.

"What do you mean?" Peter asked.

"Going after Captain Hook's treasure is dangerous! It could wind up with someone getting hurt. You could end up losing something you aren't prepared to lose. Are you sure about this?" Tootles asked. Peter squirmed, shifting his weight. He didn't like talking about things like this.

"I'm sure, Tootles. It will be an amazing adventure. Trust me," Peter brushed him off. Tootles shrugged and walked back to the helm, looking out over the sea. Peter released a deep breath. He was happy Tootles didn't push the subject anymore. The ship lurched and Peter put a hand on the rail to steady himself. He shook his head clear of the unpleasant feelings Tootles had brought up. He watched Too Small attempt to tie off a rope and fail. He sighed again.

"Tootles, I'll be in my quarters," Peter called out, walking down the staircase.

"Aye, sir!" Tootles responded. Peter walked into his cabin and shut the doors. He sank onto his bed and stared up at the ceiling, trying to figure out what he wanted to do. He was going crazy with boredom being on the ship with nothing to do. Even the Lost Boys couldn't keep him entertained. There was too much work for them to do and he didn't know what he wanted to do so anything they suggested sounded horrible.

"Captain!" Tootles called. Peter groaned and rolled over on his bed, throwing his pillow over his head. He hoped to drown out whatever squabbling was going on. He didn't want to deal with it.

"Man overboard!" Tootles yelled. There was a loud commotion outside. The crew started yelling and there was a loud splash as Peter looked up. A rope was dangling over the side of the ship. Peter sat up, surprised at the excitement happening. He got off the bed and strode out of his cabin, the double doors banging against the walls as he threw them open.

"What is going on? What is the meaning of all this?" Peter demanded. He walked over to the edge of the ship where the crew was huddled over the side. Tootles and Nibs were hauling a rope up, using every inch to get whatever was on the other end up onto the deck.

"What's happening?" Peter asked again. Nobody seemed

to be paying much attention to him. He stomped his foot, angry that nobody was answering him. A few of the boys glanced back over at him but turned away quickly.

"Too Small!" Peter snapped. Too Small jumped, then shuffled his way over to where Peter stood, disappointment on his face.

"Yes, Peter?" Too Small said, trying to glance back at what was happening.

"What is happening over there? Why is nobody answering me?" Peter asked. Too Small shrugged.

"Tootles called a man overboard. There was a dinghy off the port side. We don't really know what's happening. Only that Tootles and Nibs are bringing something up." Too Small finished. He glanced back at the group of boys again. Peter's interest peaked. This was something exciting and not at all boring. He walked past Too Small and made his way over to the side of the ship. He leaned over the edge to get a look at what was being hauled onto his ship.

"Who is that?" Peter asked, squinting to see who it was better. He couldn't tell, but he saw it was a boy. He had dark hair that covered his ears and was wearing a dark jacket and dark green khakis. Peter stepped back, waiting for the boy to approach him. Tootles and Nibs pulled him onto the deck and he stumbled a few steps before catching himself. Too Small and Slightly, a boy who thought he was smarter than everyone else, grabbed the boy's arms to make sure he didn't fall.

"Whoa. Thanks," The boy mumbled, pulling his arms free. He straightened his jacket and looked around. He ran a hand through his hair. Peter didn't know who he was or where he had come from, but he was excited. A new friend to play with - that wasn't boring at all.

"What is your name?" Peter asked, throwing his chest

out in an attempt to act like he thought a captain would. The boy looked at Peter, tilting his head.

"Jim. Jim Hawkins," The boy replied. Peter grinned, sticking his hand out.

"Peter. Peter Pan. I'm the captain," Peter explained.

"Well, Peter Pan I appreciate you and your crew rescuing me and my companion," Jim replied, shaking Peter's hand.

"Your companion?" Peter asked, looking confused and turning back to the side of the ship.

"Yes, this is Wendy," Jim explained. Peter's mouth dropped open as the girl climbed on board his ship. She smoothed out her long light blue dress and combed back her light brown hair. She flashed a brilliant and beautiful smile in Peter's direction. Peter snapped his mouth closed and gulped.

"It is truly a pleasure to meet you, sir. We don't know what we would do without you," Wendy said, advancing toward Peter. Peter backed up quickly as she held her arms out for a hug.

"Oh," Wendy said, dropping her arms and looking hurt. Peter glanced at Jim.

"You brought a girl?" Peter asked. He was completely confused as to why Jim would hang out with a girl. Everybody knew they were no fun and didn't know how to play the right way.

"Is that a problem?" Jim asked.

"Well, I just don't know why you would want to hang out with a girl," Peter replied. He crossed his arms and frowned. Jim glanced at Wendy in confusion. He looked around at the crewmembers and noticed they were staring at Wendy in awe.

"Oh!" Wendy exclaimed. She looked down as Two Small

grabbed her dress and yanked. Peter followed her gaze. He uncrossed his arms.

"Too Small!" Peter yelled. Two Small dropped his hands and looked guiltily at Peter.

"It is quite all right," Wendy said, patting Too Small on the head. Peter turned his gaze back toward her, confusion flashing over his face. Wendy smiled at him again. Peter turned on his heel and ran back into his cabin.

3

"*P*eter? Come on out!" Tootles called from outside Peter's cabin door. He knocked on the doors, the windows shaking in their frames. Peter pulled the pillow tighter over his face. Opening the door meant seeing that girl, Wendy, and he wasn't sure if he was ready for that. Tootles knocked on the doors again before giving up.

"Why would anyone want to be friends with a girl, anyway?" Peter mumbled to himself. He tossed around on his bed before jumping up and staring out the window. He watched the waves dance and play in the sunlight, spotting a few dolphins enjoying themselves. He sighed as boredom took over. He moved over to his desk and started trying to work on a plan for how they were going to get the treasure map from Captain Hook. A knock at the door, this one softer than before, surprised him.

"Oh, Peter!" Wendy's voice called out. Peter froze, hoping she would leave.

"I'm not going anywhere until you come out, Peter," Wendy called. Peter frowned, wondering if she could read his mind. He sighed again and dragged himself out of his chair. He cracked open one of the doors to his cabin and peered out with one eye.

"What do you want?" Peter demanded. Wendy's hair was blowing softly in the wind. Peter tried to remain stone-faced, but she took his breath away.

"May I come in? Please?" Wendy asked, a small smile on her lips. Peter tried to slam the door on her face, but instead, found himself opening it wider for her to walk in. He closed the door softly behind her and blinked a few times, confused as to why he had let her in. He turned around and watched her. She went straight to the back windows, watching the waves as they crashed by. She turned slowly, her eyes drifting over his bed, dresser, and the armchair. She walked over to his desk, fingers brushing softly over the plans that were sitting on top.

"Wow, you're going after Captain Hook's treasure?" Wendy asked, looking up at Peter. Her eyes were wide in awe. Peter blinked, shocked a girl knew anything about Captain Hook.

"Yes," He said, puffing his chest out, attempting to look confident. Wendy looked back down at the plans on the desk.

"Wow," She whispered. Peter took a hesitant step forward.

"How do you know about Captain Hook?" He asked. Wendy looked up, her eyebrows raised.

"Oh, I know all about him. I love pirates and the sea. I've studied all the famous pirate captains and their treasures. Captain Hook is one of the most famous pirates there is on the mainland. All in England fear him," Wendy finished. Peter tilted his head in her direction.

"I've never known a girl to like pirates," He remarked. Wendy grinned.

"I've never known a boy to be a captain," She replied. Peter grinned at her retort and folded his arms over his chest.

"I'm the youngest captain of these seas!" He exclaimed. Wendy laughed. Peter's stomach did a backflip as the sound filled the room.

"I know! You're Peter Pan, a mere boy of fourteen, captaining one of the fiercest pirate ships of all," Wendy said, plopping down in the armchair. Peter took another few steps forward, his excitement building. He uncrossed his arms.

"You've heard of me?" He asked. Wendy nodded, crossing her ankles and tucking them under the chair.

"Of course! I've always wanted to meet you. Now, not only did I meet you, but you saved me from almost certain death!" Wendy exclaimed. Peter grinned, puffing his chest out again.

"I am quite brilliant. You have to be to go after Captain Hook's treasure," Peter replied. Wendy nodded, her smile fading a little.

"Yes, that is quite a dangerous undertaking," She said. Peter's excitement started to fade and he didn't like that feeling.

"It is an adventure," Peter pushed. Wendy shrugged.

"An adventure can still be dangerous," She said. Peter thought about that for a minute.

"I guess it can be. A few of the crew members are scared to do it."

"I can imagine so. Captain Hook is a fearsome pirate. He isn't someone I would want to trifle with," Wendy responded, getting off the armchair and going back to watching the waves through the window.

"You don't think I can get his treasure?" Peter challenged her. Wendy turned around quickly.

"I didn't say that. I just said that I understand why some of the crew members may be scared to take on this adventure. It's not something to jump into lightly," Wendy argued. Peter crossed his arms again and frowned.

"What do you think I should do then?" He pushed. Wendy shrugged and turned back around.

"It's your crew, but if I was a captain, I'd talk to my crew. I'd listen to what they were scared about and figure out how to make it better for everyone."

"That's silly. Only a girl would think of something like that," Peter replied, waving her off. A knock at the door sounded before Wendy could reply.

"Come in," Peter snapped. The door opened and in stepped Jim Hawkins.

"Oh, Wendy, there you are. I was wondering where you had gotten," Jim said, stepping into the cabin and shutting the door. Peter glanced between the two of them, unsure of how he felt about having two strangers in his cabin.

"Peter, thanks again for rescuing us," Jim said, extending a hand out to Peter. Peter shook it, unsure of what else to do.

"Speaking of rescuing, why were you two stuck out there?" Peter asked, dropping Jim's hand. Wendy hesitated and looked at Jim.

"We were on a merchant ship, traveling from England around the world. Our ship was attacked by pirates and destroyed. We only survived because we had taken the lifeboat we were on to go fishing. I was the cook and needed some fresh supplies," Jim explained, rubbing a hand on the back of his neck. Peter stood up straighter.

"Pirates?" Peter asked. Jim nodded.

"It was Captain Blackbeard," Wendy replied. Jim raised his eyebrows in surprise.

"How do you know who it was?" Jim asked.

"I recognized his flags and ship," Wendy replied. Peter's excitement grew.

"You're sure it was him?" Peter asked. Wendy nodded.

"Were there any other survivors?" Peter asked. Jim shook his head.

"Honestly, we have no way of knowing, but from what we could see, no. We're the only survivors," Wendy replied. Peter nodded.

"We should get as far away from here as possible," Jim said. Peter frowned.

"Why would we do that when there's an adventure to be had?" Peter asked. It was Jim's turn to frown.

"Adventure? Pirates destroyed our entire ship and killed all of our crew. Why do you believe it would be any different for you?" Jim argued.

"Because you didn't have me aboard your ship," Peter remarked, strolling out of the cabin.

4

"*L*ads! Keep a weathered eye out on the horizon for Captain Blackbeard and his crew! Jim, what direction did you say they set sail in?" Peter asked. Jim paused on his way out of the cabin. He glanced at Wendy and shook his head.

"I didn't and I won't. I'm not going to help you sail us toward our doom," Jim replied.

"Our doom? Captain Peter would never sail us toward our doom! He has bested Captain Hook many times and always wins! Captain Blackbeard is no match for Peter Pan," Nibs cried. The rest of the crew crowed in response. Peter grinned broadly. Jim shook his head again.

"I still won't tell you. There's no point in going after him. We should get to the mainland and alert the Navy. They can take it over from there," Jim responded. Peter crossed his arms and frowned, growing impatient.

"Tell me what direction he sailed off in," Peter demanded.

"No."

"Tell me now!" Peter yelled. The lost boys started slowly

backing away from the area. None of them liked to be around Peter when he didn't get what he wanted. Jim glanced over at Wendy, frowning as he noticed the boys giving them more space.

"He went North, Peter. We don't know exactly where he was going, so he could have changed direction at any time. It's virtually impossible to find him now," Wendy said, stepping forward. Peter sighed, dropping his arms down to his sides.

"Alright, fine. We'll do it your way. Tootles, let's head to Skull Rock!" Peter commanded. The crew scrambled to get to their positions. Peter started climbing the rigging of the ship, singing obnoxiously loud.

"Yo ho! Yo ho! A pirate's life for me!"

"Peter? Oh, Peter?" Wendy called after him. Peter sang even louder and made it to the mainsail. Wendy stared up at him. He swung on a rope around the sails.

"Peter!" Jim called after him.

"Don't worry. He's done this thousands of times. He'll be okay," Tootles assured them, watching as Peter swung onto another rope. Tootles walked toward the helm and got the ship pointed toward Skull Rock. Wendy continued to watch Peter as he climbed up and down the sails and masts. Jim turned and walked over to where Tootles was standing. Jim peered out onto the water, his hands clasped behind his back.

"Wendy? Are you really a girl?" Too Small asked. Wendy looked down at him in surprise. She smiled and crouched down to his level.

"Yes, I am," Wendy replied. Too Small frowned, looking troubled.

"Peter says being around girls is no fun. He says they are no fun and don't know how to play the right way," Too Small said. Wendy frowned and straightened up. She peered up at Peter again.

"Well, we'll just have to prove him wrong, then," Wendy mumbled to herself. She walked away from Too Small, not bothering to look where she was walking. The crew scrambled around her as they went about their duties. The ship sailed along the calm waters for a few hours. Everyone passed the time by keeping the ship running as smoothly as possible. Peter spent most of it, laying on the mast, playing some windpipes. Wendy spent most of the time wandering around the ship, speaking with some of the crew members, and learning about how the ship worked. Jim spent that time on the helm, watching as the water rolled by. The sky was bright blue with no clouds.

"Captain! Skull Rock ahead!" Tootles called up to Peter. Peter jumped up, stashing his windpipes in the back of his belt. He crowed loudly and the entire crew took up the call. Peter grabbed the rope and swung to the deck.

"Peter?" Wendy called after him as she walked up. He ignored her, walking over to the helm. He turned his attention to the landmass ahead of them. Tootles handed him a telescope and Peter opened it. He pointed it toward Skull Rock and scanned the land.

The sky was dark over the island. The mountain rose up toward the sky with sharp pointed edges. It was made up of dark rock, making the whole island look like it was covered in ash. The sparse environment of trees and bushes sprinkled around the beach. The water that crashed onto the sand was harsh and chaotic. The island got its name from a cave carved into the side of the island, the shape of the rock above it carved into a skull.

Wendy walked over to stand next to Peter as he lowered the telescope. She took a deep breath as her eyes roamed over the foreboding place. Jim took a few steps closer to the edge of the ship, leaning his hands on the railing and staring out at the island.

"Peter?" Tootles called out. Peter turned around, barely able to tear his eyes away from the island.

"Yes?" Peter asked.

"Are you sure you want to do this?"

"Adventure is waiting, Tootles. Do you hear it calling?"

"Oh, Peter…" Wendy started. Peter turned to her, his eyes shining.

"Captain Hook's treasure map is somewhere on that island. We're going to find it. We're going to find his treasure," Peter replied to Wendy's unasked question. Wendy turned a frightened face toward Jim, who kept his eyes on the island.

"Jim, what do you think?" Wendy asked, stepping closer to him. She wasn't going to let him avoid this discussion.

"I refused to give the location of Captain Blackbeard because I thought we would be sailing toward our doom. It turns out, we ended up sailing there anyway," Jim muttered. His voice was bitter and harsh. Wendy turned around, looking around for support. She spotted Too Small on the lower deck.

"Too Small! You can't support this. Do you?" Wendy cried, desperation clinging to her voice. Too Small stuttered and glanced around in panic.

"I…uh, I don't know…n-not really," Too Small stuttered. Wendy turned back to Peter.

"There! See that? Too Small doesn't support this either," Wendy argued. Peter turned to Too Small.

"Is this true?" Peter asked, his voice eerily calm.

"N-no…y-yes, well, the rest of the crew…" Too Small stumbled over his words. Peter raised his eyebrows.

"Well? Which is it?" Peter asked, keeping his voice low. Too Small cleared his throat and glanced over at his crew members.

"None of us think this is a good idea, Captain," Too Small mumbled. Peter looked around at everyone, surprised.

"None of who?" Peter asked.

"Everyone," Nibs offered, his courage building as he talked. He walked a few steps up the staircase and pointed toward the island.

"That island looks spooky, Peter. It's not welcoming. It doesn't want us there. Plus, Captain Hook will come after us if we take his treasure. It's not a good idea," Nibs continued. Peter looked from crew member to crew member. They all shuffled backward and lowered their gaze as he looked at them.

"So, that's how everyone feels, is it?" Peter asked. Nobody answered him. Peter turned to Tootles.

"Tootles, is this how you feel?" Peter asked him politely. Tootles sighed and rubbed a hand on the back of his neck.

"Cap, I'm gonna be honest. It doesn't look good, but you're my captain. I will follow you wherever you order, whether it looks good or not," Tootles replied. Jim pushed off the edge of the ship and walked toward Peter.

"You'll doom us all if you go after Captain Hook's treasure," Jim sneered. Peter grinned.

"Luckily, you're not the captain, Mr. Hawkins. I am! I'm ready for an adventure. We're already here. We might as well go in," Peter said, gesturing to the island. Jim rolled his eyes.

"Enjoy your funeral," He spat. Peter stepped in front of him as he started to walk away.

"Oh, but Mr. Hawkins, you're coming with us," Peter said. Jim's mouth dropped open.

"I most certainly am not!" Jim exclaimed. Peter grinned, stepping back.

"Tootles, would you be so kind as to help Wendy and Jim into the lifeboats?" Peter asked. Tootles stepped forward and took Jim and Wendy by the arms. Jim started immediately shouting and yelling. Peter turned to Too Small.

"Too Small, gather the rest of the lost boys, and get into the lifeboats. We are going to shore now!" Peter instructed. Too Small squeaked and then hurried to follow Peter's directions. Peter turned back to the island, his excitement growing as he realized how close he was to getting Captain Hook's treasure. He walked over to the edge of the ship, watching as everyone piled into the boats. He crowed loudly and jumped into the lifeboat. It was lowered into the water and they took off.

5

The boys pulled the lifeboats up onto the shore, flopping down on the warm sand in exhaustion. Peter jumped off the boat and scampered around the beach, pointing and exclaiming at every living thing he saw. Wendy watched as he ran, the way a mother would watch her child as they experienced something new.

"Hasn't he been here before?" Wendy asked Tootles. Tootles sat up and turned to watch Peter. He nodded.

"Aye, hundreds of times," Tootles responded. Wendy frowned.

"Why does he act as if he's never seen anything on this island then?" She asked.

"It's Peter," Tootles shrugged and stood up. He started getting the rest of the crew members to their feet and directing them to follow after Peter. Wendy glanced at Jim, who was frowning in Peter's direction.

"There's something not right about that boy," Jim muttered. Wendy sighed. She knew something was wrong with Peter, but she couldn't figure out how to help him. Peter climbed a few trees, laughing as coconuts fell below, almost hitting several of the crew members. Wendy frowned, watching all this happen.

"Peter! Somebody could get hurt. Stop that right now," Wendy called after him. Peter paused, looking at her. He climbed down the tree and crossed his arms.

"This is why we don't bring girls," Peter said, looking at Jim. Jim blinked, glancing over at Wendy. Wendy's face went bright red and she marched up to Peter.

"Girls are just as much fun as boys. Just because we try not to get hurt doesn't mean we don't know how to have fun on adventures," Wendy said, jabbing a finger at Peter's chest. Peter took a surprised step back and then drew the short knife that was tucked in his waist. His face darkened, an evil grin spreading. Wendy gasped, stumbling back.

"Do you dare challenge me to a duel?" Peter exclaimed, jabbing the knife in Wendy's direction a few times. Wendy shuffled a few steps back, fear crossing her face. Jim took a few steps toward them. He wasn't sure how to help, but he knew that he should. Tootles grabbed his arm and held him back. Jim frowned in confusion and Tootles held a hand up.

"Peter! Which way to the treasure map?" Tootles called out. Peter froze and then perked up in Tootles' direction. His face lightened and he crowed loudly for all to hear. He sprang toward Tootles, laughing loudly as he ran.

"This way! The map is this way, men! Follow me!" Peter shouted, dancing and jumping into the forest. Peter shoved the knife back into his waist, laughing as he went. Jim walked over to Wendy and threw an arm around her. They stood there, silently, watching as all the lost boys followed Peter into the forest. Tootles walked over to where Jim and Wendy stood.

"This is Peter's world. You never tell Peter what to do. Peter does what he wants and we all follow him. There is no arguing. If Peter becomes bored of you or doesn't think you'll play what he wants, he'll end up leaving you for the pirates...or worse," Tootles explained. He walked off, slowly following after Peter and the crew. Wendy looked at Jim.

"What does he mean by worse?" Wendy whispered. Jim gulped, trying to get rid of the shake in his voice.

"I don't think we should find out," Jim responded. He steered Wendy toward the trail into the forest and they followed the noises of the crew. They walked on for a while, not saying much. Every once in a while, they stopped hearing the yelling and crowing from the lost boys. Wendy swatted away flies that buzzed near her ears. Jim wiped the sweat off his forehead over and over again. It went on this way for what felt like forever to Jim and Wendy. Suddenly, Wendy blinked, looking around her.

"Jim, hasn't it gone awfully quiet?" Wendy asked. Jim stopped and looked around in surprise.

"Yes, it has. I wonder what that's all about," Jim remarked, taking a step forward. A bush rustled from their left. Jim motioned for Wendy to stay quiet, as he stepped toward the bush. The bush on the right started rustling. A twig cracked. Wendy's heart pounded in her chest.

"Boo!" Peter yelled in her ear. She screamed and jumped. Peter's laughter was loud and boisterous, echoing around the trees. The twins popped up from the bushes that had rustled, scaring Jim in the process. The rest of the lost boys popped out of their hiding places, Nibs swinging upside from the tree branch above them. They all joined in on the laughter.

"That was a fun game!" Peter clapped his hands. Wendy stomped her foot.

"That was not nice, Peter," Wendy said. Peter just smiled at her and didn't bother to say anything.

"You gave us quite a fright, mate. We thought you were some pirates or man-eating monster," Jim said sportingly. He grinned in pain, attempting to smooth the situation over while getting his heart rate under control.

"Wouldn't that have been awesome? A band of pirates jumping out and attacking you!" Peter exclaimed. He mimicked some sword-fighting movements and jumped around Wendy and Jim.

"Well, we don't have any swords. We wouldn't be able to join in on the fight," Jim answered him. Wendy stared at Peter in disbelief. Peter turned around and frowned.

"That's not right. We must get you some weapons. How else will you help us raid if you don't have weapons?"

"Raid?" Wendy repeated.

"Tootles! Get them weapons. The raid begins at sundown!" Peter yelled, turning on his heel and jumping away. Wendy and Jim exchanged worried glances. Tootles walked up to them, carrying two different weapons. He handed Jim a long sword with a brass hilt. He handed Wendy a small dagger with a black handle.

"What do we do with these?" Wendy asked, holding the dagger away from her body.

"Keep it with you at all times. You never know when you might need it," Tootles explained. Wendy looked at him in alarm.

"Why would I need it?" She asked, her voice tight. Tootles shrugged.

"Peter might want to duel, pirates attack you, the Many-More could show up, or you could walk into a trap set by the fairies. Who knows what might happen?" Tootles said, turning and following Peter. The lost boys laughed at

Wendy and Jim, climbing in the trees and running down the trail.

"What is a ManyMore?" Jim asked. He watched Peter stop and turn around, waiting for them to catch up. He had a serious face, but Jim didn't trust the way his eyes looked.

"The ManyMore is the monster on the Jolly Roger island. It doesn't have a real name. We call it the ManyMore because no matter how many sacrifices we give it, it will always want many more. It never stops being hungry. It never stops wanting to feed. It is a shapeless, soulless, bottomless black pit. If it comes near you, you're done for," Peter said, his voice getting quieter as he went on speaking. Wendy felt chills go down her arms and spine. She shivered as Peter grinned.

"Peter! The raid?" Tootles asked. Peter turned around and skipped away.

"The raid! The raid! We're gonna raid! Watch out, pirates, here we come to raid!" Peter sang. Tootles walked over to Wendy and Jim.

"Keep to the back. Peter and the rest of the boys will take care of the pirates. You shouldn't need to get involved at all. Although, keep a sharp eye out. Sometimes the pirates end up getting past a boy and may end up going straight for you," Tootles warned them. They nodded.

"Does Peter know where the map is?" Wendy asked. Tootles smirked.

"Of course. He steals it on a regular basis. The pirates always hide it in the same exact spot," Tootles replied.

"That doesn't seem very smart," Wendy frowned. Tootles shrugged.

"We can't know why the pirates do what they do."

Tootles turned and followed after the lost boys, jogging to catch up. Wendy and Jim walked slowly down the trail, keeping a sharp eye out for pirates. They didn't meet any along the way, but they caught glimpses of them. A flash of clothing in the forest, some unfortunate previous victims of the pirates, and a few swords were all strewn along the sides of the trail.

6

"*W*hat happened to Wendy and Jim?" Nibs asked Tootles. Tootles glanced behind them in surprise. He sighed, wiping a hand down his face.

"The pirates got them! We must rescue them! Another big adventure!" Peter yelled, pulling his knife from his belt and thrusting it into the air. The lost boys followed his lead and soon all the swords were pointing toward the sky. Peter crowed and led the charge into the pirates camp. There was just one problem.

There were no pirates to be found.

"Search everywhere! They're here. I know it!" Peter commanded. The lost boys spread out and searched high and low. They pulled tent flaps back and boarded the ship that was tethered to the dock. They pulled back rocks and looked up in the trees. It didn't matter where they looked. The pirates were nowhere to be found. Wendy and Jim came walking into the camp, looking around the area in surprise.

"Peter, what happened to all the pirates?" Nibs asked,

the bravest of the bunch. Peter frowned, not liking this game very much.

"Peter!" Tootles called, pointing. Peter walked over to where Tootles was standing and looked at what he was pointing at. He saw all the pirates walking along the trail, their eye patches and peg legs keeping their pace slow. He watched as they cut brush and tree limbs from their path and his anger grew.

"They changed the rules of the game. That's not how this game goes," Peter muttered under his breath. All the lost boys took a step back, glancing at each other in fear. They didn't want to be near Peter when he got angry.

"They changed the rules!" Peter screamed, swinging his sword around wildly. He caught some of the ropes keeping the tents up, which caused them to crumble. A few branches from unlucky nearby trees went flying as Peter's sword chopped them off.

"You two!" Peter screamed wildly, as he turned on Wendy and Jim. He pointed his sword at them, his eyes wide.

"What about us?" Wendy responded with a frown. She refused to let this boy intimidate and blame them for something they hadn't done. She crossed her arms. Peter advanced, his sword pointed straight at her heart. He almost impaled her until Tootles' sword blocked him. Peter looked at Tootles, the anger clear on his face. Tootles stared calmly back, not saying anything.

"You dare challenge me?" Peter snarled.

"Nope. I'm not challenging anybody," Tootles replied. Peter narrowed his eyes and pulled his sword back.

"Then, why would you protect these swine?" He asked. Wendy scoffed.

"Swine? Swine? I'll have you know that I am Wendy

Darling. Nobody calls me swine. Least of all some boy who doesn't know how to behave. Swine. Ha! That is just laughable," Wendy wagged her finger at Peter, advancing on him while she was yelling. Peter stumbled back a few steps, surprised. He quickly recovered and swung his sword up again. Wendy slapped it away, jabbing Peter in the chest.

"No. You don't get to be a bully. You need to stop being so mean to people who don't do what you want them to do," Wendy snapped. Peter frowned. Tootles stepped between them quickly.

"Peter, why don't we go find the map? The treasure waits for no one, remember?" Tootles suggested. He glanced at Wendy and turned Peter around. It took a few minutes, but Peter eventually focused on finding the map. The lost boys collectively let loose breath and started wandering around the camp. They searched the tents and the ship, exclaiming when they found something they were interested in. The twins found a bear they fought over until the stuffing exploded everywhere.

"Peter, do you know where the map is?" Tootles asked. Peter puffed his chest out and laughed loudly.

"Of course I do. It's in the captain's quarters," Peter boasted. He walked with importance onto the ship and across the deck. He didn't even wait for Tootles to follow him. All of the boys Peter passed bowed and stepped out of his way. He threw open the cabin doors and strutted in. He ignored the jewelry laying in the cabinet along the wall. He didn't even glance at the velvet blankets on the large bed. He focused his gaze on the picture behind the large desk. It was a painting of a ship on the turbulent ocean.

"The map is in there?" Jim asked, sounding confused. Peter whirled around.

"What are you doing here? You can't see this!" Peter exclaimed.

"Well, it's too late now. I've already seen it," Jim shrugged. Peter frowned, sighing.

"Alright, but you can't tell anyone. Okay?" Peter asked. Jim nodded.

"No, you have to pinky swear," Peter insisted.

"Pinky swear?"

"Yes. It's the only way to make sure you don't tell anyone," Peter responded. He held out his pinky. Jim sighed and looped his with Peter's. Peter grinned.

"Alright, I pinky swear."

"Awesome!" Peter exclaimed, dropping Jim's pinky. He turned around and pulled at the painting. The right side swung out from the wall and behind it was a safe. Jim whistled.

"Impressive."

"I know."

Peter reached forward and input the combination. Jim watched intently, committing the numbers to memory - 17 47 98 46. The safe swung open. Peter and Jim peered intently into it, not saying a word. They stayed like that for a few moments, until Jim pulled back and cleared his throat.

"Uh...are you sure the map was here?" Jim asked. Peter turned around, his face blank. Jim took a step back, unsure of what to say. Peter walked out of the cabin. Tootles passed him, giving him a funny look as he walked by. Tootles walked up to Jim, glancing in the safe behind him.

"Where's the map?" Tootles asked. Jim cleared his throat again.

"It wasn't in there," Jim responded. Tootles stiffened.

"What?"

"The map is gone."

"That's impossible."

"Is it though? I mean from what you have said and how Peter's been acting, the pirates have been putting everything in the exact same place every time. It seems like they've had enough of you raiding them," Jim shrugged. Tootles shook his head slowly.

"This is not going to go well," Tootles mumbled. Jim shrugged.

"What's Peter going to do? It's not like he can control everything that happens on this island," Jim responded. Tootles didn't respond. Thankfully, the weird silence was interrupted by Nibs and the twins walking into the cabin.

"What's going on? Peter just walked off the ship without sharing a look at the map. What gives?" Nibs demanded, crossing his arms. Tootles just stared at him.

"There is no map," Jim explained. Nibs yelped, covering his eyes and the twins glanced at each other in worry.

"Why is that such a big deal?" Jim asked. Tootles ran a hand down his face.

"Do you remember the reaction Peter had to the pirates not being here when they should have been?" Tootles asked. Jim nodded.

"Of course."

"Well, let's just say this is worse," Tootles explained.

"Oh, dear," Jim whispered. Tootles nodded.

"Now you understand."

"Wendy!" Jim exclaimed, rushing out of the cabin. He ran across the ship deck and off the ramp. He searched the camp, but she wasn't anywhere to be found. Peter was also gone.

"Where would he take her?" Jim asked Tootles. Tootles looked surprised and stuttered for a minute.

"I-I'm not really sure. This is all new - for all of us. He's never gone off the deep end like this because everything has been predictable before this," Tootles explained. Jim pulled at his hair in frustration.

"What about Mermaid Lagoon?" Nibs offered.

"No way! He'd take her to Crocodile Creek Cove," One of the twins interjected.

"Like you'd know anything. He took her to the pirates to trade her for the map," The other twin argued. Jim looked around in a panic, not understanding a word the boys were saying, but sure none of those places would bode well for Wendy. He started to freak out. Tootles called around, gathering all of the lost boys.

"What's going on, Tootles?" One of the boys asked. Tootles heaved a big sigh and told them what was happening.

"The map is gone?"

"The map isn't there?"

"Where is the map?"

The boys started asking question after question. Tootles got them to settle down. He explained everything they knew at that point. He asked the boys if they had seen Peter and Wendy take off and what direction they headed in. Of course, none of the boys had the same answer. Each boy pointed in a different direction. Some of them said Peter and Wendy went together. Others said they went in opposite directions.

"This is hopeless. Wendy is probably dead, run through by Peter's knife," Jim wailed. Tootles grabbed his shoulder and shook him roughly.

"Don't give up just yet."

7

"I've found it!" Too Small cried. He waved a scroll in the air, excitement covering his face. He scrambled back over to where all of the boys were standing around. They crowded around him, eager to see what he had found. When he unrolled the scroll, a collective gasp went through the boys.

"Too Small, you've found Captain Hook's treasure map!" Tootles exclaimed.

"Where did you find it?" Nibs asked. Too Small crossed his arms.

"No way. I'm not telling you. You'll take credit for finding it," Too Small said, sticking his tongue out. Nibs drew his sword.

"Why, you no good scoundrel! How dare you accuse me of thievery? You are the worst of the worst. Prepare to die," Nibs snarled. Too Small drew his sword as well, holding the hilt with both hands.

"Nobody is going to die today. We have to find Peter and tell him we found the map," Tootles interrupted the fight. Too Small stuck his sword back in his belt. After a moment,

Nibs scowled and did the same. Tootles started ordering the boys around. He directed them to split up into pairs and search for Peter.

"Peter!" Too Small called out.

"Peter! I've found the map!" Nibs called even louder. Too Small shoved him.

"No, you haven't. I did it!" Too Small argued. The boys fell to the ground, wrestling and shouting about who actually found the map. They made it out of the pirate's camp and down into the forest a little ways. As they rolled around on the ground, they hit something solid. It wasn't as hard as a log, but it wasn't a bush that gave way to their wrestling. Too Small looked up to see Peter standing there.

"Peter!" Too Small cried. He scrambled off of Nibs and saluted Peter. Peter returned the salute, grinning.

"You said you found the map?" Peter asked, watching Nibs scramble to his feet.

"I found it, Peter. It was me!" Nibs insisted. Too Small elbowed Nibs in the ribs.

"Oh, yeah? Where did you find it then?" Too Small asked, crossing his arms.

"Uh...well, behind a tree...near the edge of the camp," Nibs fibbed. Too Small narrowed his eyes.

"Where is it?" Peter asked, his excitement growing.

"With Tootles," Too Small explained. Peter took off running, laughing as he swung from branches and ducked under bushes. Too Small and Nibs did their best to keep up with him, but he was just too fast. Peter easily beat them back to camp.

"Where is Wendy?" Jim demanded when he spotted Peter. Nibs and Too Small joined the group, watching everything unfold. Peter was too busy looking at the map to answer Jim. Tootles stood in front of Peter with his hands on his hips, watching Peter's expressions.

"Did you kill her? Is she okay?" Jim tried again. Peter looked up at Tootles, excitement in his eyes.

"Onward! To treasure!" Peter exclaimed, rolling up the map and thrusting it into the air. The lost boys all cheered and started the long trek back to their ship. Peter started to follow them until Jim grabbed his arm and pulled him back.

"Answer me. I need to know!" Jim wailed. Peter looked confused and annoyed.

"Need to know what?" Peter asked. Jim glanced at Tootles in despair.

"Where is Wendy? What did you do with her?"

"Who is Wendy?"

"The girl, Peter. Where is the girl?" Tootles stepped in, as Jim crumpled to the ground. Tears streamed down his face. Peter frowned, thinking.

"Oh! The angry one? I put her back on the ship. I didn't want to play with her anymore," Peter shrugged. Jim gasped, taking in a deep breath and standing up.

"So, she's okay?" Jim asked, his voice full of hope. Peter looked surprised.

"Of course!" Peter responded. Tootles didn't look as convinced.

"You didn't leave her for the ManyMore?" Tootles accused Peter. Jim's face morphed into a look of horror. Peter frowned.

"Why would I do that? The ManyMore is satisfied with the offering I made to it," Peter responded. Jim choked out a sob.

"What offering would that be, Peter?" Tootles demanded to know. Peter grinned and leaned in as if he was telling Tootles a secret.

"Wouldn't you like to know?" Peter whispered. He laughed loudly and then took off after the lost boys. Tootles sighed, rubbing a hand on the back of his neck.

"Well, that's Peter for you," He muttered. Jim looked up at him, slowly standing up.

"That's all you have to say? What about Wendy?" Jim demanded. Tootles shook his head.

"There's a chance she's on the ship, but I wouldn't put it past Peter to have given her to the ManyMore. If he did, there's nothing you can do," Tootles said, putting a hand on Jim's shoulder. Jim roughly shoved it off, glaring at Tootles. Tootles shrugged and started down the trail. Jim looked around the pirate camp miserably, tears running down his face.

"Oh, Wendy. I do hope you're on that ship when I get there," Jim muttered miserably, as he turned and followed after everyone. Jim followed the trial, not bothering to catch up with the lost boys. They were all too happy for him to be around. He wanted to sulk in his misery. He focused on the ground in front of him, tuning out all of the sounds in front of him.

"Jim Hawkins!" Peter yelled in Jim's face. Jim came to a sudden halt, looking up in alarm. Peter was standing in front of him, his hands on his hips and a triumphant look on his face.

"What do you want?" Jim asked. He started walking again, not bothering to walk around Peter. Peter ended up moving out of Jim's way, following after him.

"What's wrong, Jim? Don't you want to play?" Peter asked. Jim stopped and turned on his heel.

"No, I don't want to play. I want to get off this cruddy island and find someone who isn't a complete psycho to take me home. I want to find Wendy and I want nothing more to do with you," Jim spat in Peter's face. Peter took a step back, confused.

"Why don't you like me, Jim?" Peter asked. Jim stared at him, not saying a word. He turned on his heel and continued walking, not bothering to answer Peter's question. Peter followed after him, bouncing around, repeating his question.

"Peter, we need to get in the lifeboats now. The tide is coming in," Tootles called out. Jim stepped out from between two trees and felt the warm sand slip into his shoes. He sighed, exhaustion starting to come over his body. He made his way into the closest boat, not bothering to even ask. The boats were loaded and pushed off into the tide. Peter had chosen to sit in the other lifeboat, playing a game of tic tac toe with Too Small. Jim kept his eyes on the ship, praying he would see Wendy again.

They made it to the ship quickly, the current making their journey relatively easy. They started to climb up the side of the ship, one by one. Jim waited for a few of the lost boys to go up first. He had to gather his courage to face what was up there. He jumped in front of Nibs and scrambled up the rope ladder. He made it to the deck and looked around wildly.

No sign of Wendy anywhere.

"Wendy?" Jim called out. He was starting to panic and tears were threatening to make their way down his face again. As soon as Peter stepped on deck, Jim stomped up to him.

"You said Wendy was on the ship," Jim snapped. Peter blinked, glancing at Tootles.

"Did I?" Peter asked, unsure of what was happening. Jim groaned and started calling out for Wendy again. Tootles glanced toward Jim and then stepped closer to Peter. He put a hand under his arm and guided him to the captain's chambers. He opened the doors and guided Peter into the cabin.

"Alright, Peter, tell me. What did you do with Wendy?" Tootles sighed. Peter just grinned.

"Wouldn't you like to know?" Peter taunted him. Tootles rubbed the bridge of his nose.

"Don't make me do something you're not going to like, Peter," Tootles warned him. Peter crossed his arms with a smile on his face.

"Like what?" Peter dared him. Tootles dropped his hand and stared at Peter. He nodded and walked out of the cabin, leaving the doors open. Peter followed after him, standing in the doorway.

"Crew! Listen up! Anyone caught playing with Peter instead of at their position will be thrown in the brig. A second offense will result in immediate dismissal from this ship. Do I make myself clear?" Tootles asked, looking around at every face. They all looked serious, nodding at Tootles. Peter stomped his foot and walked out to Tootles.

"That's not fair! I want to play a game," Peter argued.

"Not until you tell me where the girl is," Tootles replied, his voice calm. Peter scoffed and folded his arms. He rolled his eyes.

"She's aloft," Peter muttered. Tootles' eyes traveled upward, looking at the mast. Jim's eyes followed, a gasp escaping his lips as he noticed what Tootles was looking at. Wendy was tied to the mast, in the crow's nest. Her mouth was covered with a rag of some type. Jim immediately turned to look at Peter.

"Why did you do that?" He demanded. Peter broke out into a smile.

"Because it's fun! Don't you think so?" Peter asked.

39

Tootles shook his head, not bothering to look at Peter. Jim glanced between the two of them.

"How are we supposed to get her down? How did you even get her up there?" Jim asked, covering his eyes with his hands. Peter grinned.

"It was a fun game. She climbed at the point of a sword," Peter clapped his hands. Jim wailed loudly. Tootles sighed, turning to address the rest of the crew.

"Alright, lads. Help the poor girl down," Tootles instructed them. The boys climbed quickly, reaching Wendy in record time. Tootles and Jim watched her get untied and then be led along the yardarm. She started the climb down, the boys swinging from ropes and scaling the ladder alongside her.

"That wasn't very fun, Tootles," Peter said, his voice dark and dangerous. Tootles turned around, his face neutral.

"You had your fun, Peter," Tootles replied. Jim glanced between the two of them. Peter turned on his heel and stomped into his cabin. He slammed the doors closed. Tootles sighed, rubbing a hand down his face.

"Do you two always fight?" Jim asked. Tootles frowned.

"That's not a fight. Besides, it doesn't matter what you say. Peter always wins," Tootles replied.

"That must be hard," Jim replied. Tootles shrugged. He watched Wendy make her way down the rigging and step lightly onto the deck. Jim's face flooded with relief as he rushed up to wrap her in a hug.

"Where is he?" Wendy demanded, untangling herself from Jim's embrace and stomping up to Tootles. Tootles raised his eyebrows but didn't say anything. He lifted his arm and pointed at the captain's cabin. Wendy growled and stomped over. She grabbed both door handles and threw the doors open.

"CAPTAIN PETER! Might I have a word with you?" Wendy shouted as she marched into the cabin. Tootles and Jim exchanged a glance. The entire crew slowed to a halt and watched the cabin doors. There was complete silence for a few minutes. Tootles glanced around and frowned. He clapped his hands.

"Back to work, you scurvy dogs!" Tootles shouted. The boys ran back to their positions.

8

"Just what do you think you were doing, Peter?" Wendy demanded, crossing her arms. Peter stared at her from his corner, his eyes wide in surprise. She moved closer to him. He didn't even flinch. She scowled.

"Answer me, Peter," Wendy said, her temper diminishing slowly. Peter blinked a few times, taking a step forward.

"What are you doing?" Peter asked. Wendy frowned, noting Peter's voice was soft and hesitant.

"What are you talking about? I'm yelling at you for tying me up to the sail," Wendy replied. Her confusion was taking over her feelings of anger. Peter took another few steps forward.

"It was a fun game. Why are you yelling?" Peter asked. Wendy scoffed and rolled her eyes.

"It wasn't fun for me! It was terrifying. Especially since you left me alone up there!" Wendy threw her hands up. Peter frowned.

"That's just because girls don't know how to play," Peter remarked. Wendy narrowed her eyes at him.

"Girls know how to play better than boys. In fact, I know how to play better than *you*," Wendy countered. Peter crossed his arms and stomped his foot.

"NO! No, you don't!"

"Yes, I do. I know how to play the best."

"You're lying!" Peter screamed. Wendy let loose a dull laugh.

"No, I'm not."

"Prove it."

"Tell me how," Wendy responded. Peter frowned, thinking. He turned around to look at the water. Wendy followed his gaze. She enjoyed the feeling of the boat dipping into the waves under her feet. She noticed something out of the corner of her eye on her left. She turned to look and realized there was a ship outside the window.

"Peter?" Wendy asked, not bothering to look at him. He ignored her, trying to figure out the perfect way to prove that he was the best at playing.

"Peter!" Wendy shouted. Peter started to turn toward her, but she tackled him to the ground. A cannonball ripped through the cabin, right where Peter's head had been. Wood flew over Wendy and Peter, while a bell went off in alarm. Wendy groaned, moving some of the broken plywood off of her body. She looked down at Peter.

"Peter? Are you okay?" Wendy asked. She shook his shoulder, looking around her. She noticed the ship was starting to make its way around the other side of their ship. She pushed more wood off of her, getting to her knees. She was starting to panic. She reached over and shook Peter again.

"Peter! There are pirates!" Wendy cried. Peter's eyes flew open and he smiled.

"Pirates?" He asked, sitting up, not bothering to move any of the wood that covered his body. It fell away as he stood up and stared at the ship sailing past his window. He looked down at Wendy, his eyes sparkling.

"Pirates!" He exclaimed, thrusting a fist in the air. He jumped out of the pile of wood that lay at their feet. The ocean breeze started coming in, lifting Peter's light brown hair. He pulled open the doors to a cabinet with both hands. He leaned in and started rummaging around. Wendy frowned, getting to her feet. She planted her hands on her hips.

"You're happy about this?" She asked. Peter paused and turned to look at her.

"Yes! There are pirates. It's time for Battle!" Peter cried, pulling two swords out of the cabinet. Wendy gasped, a hand flying up to her mouth.

"Battle? You mean to the death?" Wendy asked.

"How else would you play battle?" Peter frowned. Wendy scoffed.

"With wooden swords? So nobody gets hurt," Wendy responded. Peter rolled his eyes.

"That is for little babies. Boys aren't worried about getting hurt. That's part of the fun! It's part of the adventure," Peter responded. He threw a sword at Wendy. She yelped, grabbing for the handle as it flew toward her. It clattered to the floor. Wendy picked it up hesitantly, looking back up at Peter in embarrassment. She didn't need to worry, because he had already lifted his sword above his head and ran out of his cabin with a war cry.

"This is crazy," Wendy muttered. She held the sword at her side, moving toward the cabin doors. Another cannonball blasted through the ship, making it rock unsteadily under her feet. She spread her arms out to keep her balance. She took a step closer to the doors that were swinging wildly. She pulled one open and held it to the wall. Her mouth dropped as she took in the sight on the deck.

"Get him, Nibs!" Peter screamed. Wendy watched Nibs swing his sword above his head and straight down onto a large man's neck. The man screamed as the sword cut through his skin and blood went spraying everywhere. Peter clapped his hands, laughing as the man fell to the ground. Nibs turned to a pirate who was rushing up to him, his sword in front. Wendy looked to her right. Jim was fighting with a large pirate, who's large gut was swinging and causing him to lose his balance every so often.

"Jim, sweep the leg!" Wendy called out. Jim glanced in her direction and then looked at the pirate's legs. The pirate glanced at Wendy, taking his attention off of Jim. As he turned back, Jim stuck his sword through his belly, then kicked him square in the chest. The pirate stumbled back, holding the cut in his stomach, and then fell flat on his back. Wendy flinched. She took a step out of the cabin.

"Way to go, Wendy!" Peter exclaimed. Wendy glanced over at him, noting he was currently locked in a fight with three nasty looking pirates. One was extremely tall, his long limbs making it easier to get closer to Peter. He had a red bandana wrapped around his head. One of them was shorter - almost as short as Too Small. His brown shorts reached his ankles. The last pirate made Wendy double take.

"C-captain Hook," Wendy whispered in awe and fear. Peter laughed, lunging forward and attempting to drive his sword through Captain Hook's stomach.

"Missed, my boy! Want to try again?" Captain Hook exclaimed, looking gleeful as he returned Peter's advances.

"Of course, Captain! It'd be my honor," Peter said, crossing his sword over his chest and bowing low to the ground. Captain Hook raised his sword, swiping down at Peter's head.

"Peter! Look out!" Wendy cried, her hands rising to her mouth. Peter looked up at her and grinned, winking. He took a step to the left and Captain Hook's sword struck the deck.

"Why, you nasty little boy!" Captain Hook cried. Peter laughed loudly. He ran over to the edge of the ship, jumped up on the hull, and grabbed onto the shroud next to him. Wendy reached out to him, panic starting to envelop her. Captain Hook sneered, pointing his sword at Peter.

"I'll get you, Peter Pan! If it's the last thing I do!" Captain Hook swore.

9

*P*eter grinned as Captain Hook approached him. He crowed loudly, causing Captain Hook to pause. The crew answered his call, the boys crowing themselves. Peter laughed again and then leaned backward, letting go of the shroud.

"Hang on, Peter! You'll fall into the water!" Wendy cried, lifting her own sword and running to help Peter out. Captain Hook turned on her. She stopped in her tracks, taking in his full form. He had on a long, dark red coat. She could see some areas were darker and gulped, realizing that was blood. She hoped it wasn't from any of the boys. Her eyes traveled to his hand, taking in the sharp, silver hook at the end of his arm. It flashed in the bright sunlight. Wendy's eyes traveled to his face, where a wicked grin was waiting to greet her. It was framed by large, black curly hair, which was topped with a very flamboyant black hat. There was a white feather sticking out of it.

"Hello, my dear. I'm surprised to see you here," Captain Hook said, his voice smooth and dangerous. Wendy took a step back, whimpering as she realized her mistake.

"Why?" She managed to ask. Captain Hook looked surprised.

"Why, because you're a girl, of course! The last girl Peter came into contact with, he killed," Captain Hook laughed. Wendy's eyes widened and her mouth dropped open.

"Really?" She whispered. Captain Hook smiled, a twinkle in his eye.

"Oh, yes. All she wanted to do was play, but she couldn't play the right way. Therefore, Peter had to get rid of her. Otherwise, she would have ruined his perfect game. She would have stood in the way of his treasure," Captain Hook purred. He took a few cautious steps forward, his confidence gaining when Wendy didn't react. She was stuck in her own head, her thoughts spinning.

"What treasure is so important?" Wendy demanded to know. She lowered her sword, frowning as she thought over what Captain Hook was telling her. Captain Hook sly smile hid secrets.

"You don't know?" He asked. Wendy shook her head.

"As you said, I'm a girl. He thinks I don't play the right way. He doesn't want me on the ship," Wendy replied. She lowered her head, tears springing to her eyes. Captain Hook tsked his tongue, a sympathetic noise coming from him as he moved closer to Wendy.

"That must be so hard," He said. Wendy wiped her eyes. Captain Hook wrapped his arm around her shoulders.

"You must be so upset. Come, sit with me awhile," Captain Hook suggested. Wendy shrugged and agreed, letting herself be steered back into the captain's cabin. The doors shut behind her, shutting out the noise of the fighting still going on. Captain Hook guided her to the chair behind the desk. She flopped down, dropping the sword on the desk. Captain Hook wrapped his hands behind his back, his sword sticking up over one shoulder. He roamed around the cabin, letting his eyes wander around each item Peter had collected.

"How long have you known, Peter?" Captain Hook asked, his tone light. Wendy sniffed, wiping her eyes.

"Not very long at all. He rescued Jim and me from our lifeboat. Our ship got attacked by pirates and sunk," Wendy replied. Captain Hook nodded, sympathetically.

"I can only imagine how scary that must have been. And now, to have to deal with it again? You must be exhausted," Captain Hook suggested. Wendy paused, taking stock of her body and what it was saying to her. She sighed heavily.

"I am exhausted," Wendy replied, sinking into the back of the chair.

"Why don't you rest? Don't trouble yourself with what's happening out there. It's for silly boys to deal with. You have yourself a nice rest in here," Captain Hook suggested. Wendy bit her lip, glancing at the doors.

"I don't know...the boys might need me. They are awfully young and with Peter overboard, they probably don't know what to do. They probably need somebody to lead them," Wendy muttered, starting to get out of the chair. Captain Hook eased her back into the chair.

"They're fine. They've been doing this far longer than you've been on board. Besides, they have Tootles. They can last a few minutes without you," He soothed her. She sighed again, her eyes fluttering closed.

"I suppose."

"Do you, by any chance, happen to know where Peter hid that pesky treasure map?" Captain Hook said, keeping his voice light and as nonchalant as he could. Wendy's eyes flew open. She sat up straighter, doing her best not to alert Captain Hook of the change in her attitude.

"Uh...no. He never showed it to me. I'm a girl and not very good at playing, remember? He tied me up in the crow's nest and left me there while everyone was making their way back to the boats," Wendy replied, shifting slightly in her seat. She looked at the mirror hanging on the wall in front of her. She noted Captain Hook's head turned in her direction when she shifted. She knew he was watching her much more closely than he seemed. She silently cursed herself for letting him lull her into this situation.

"How did you two get back on the ship without a lifeboat?" Captain Hook asked. He raised an eyebrow at the back of her head. She watched in the mirror as he twirled the sword around with his good hand. She gulped.

"I...I don't really remember. I remember him tugging me through your camp and across the island. We went really fast and I kept falling. He got me to the edge of the island and I yanked my arm out of his grip. I told him I wasn't going to go with him. I wanted to wait for Jim and the rest of the boys. He gave me a really scary smile and then snapped his fingers. The next thing I knew, I was in the crow's nest. Peter was finishing tying the knots around my feet. He looked up at me and smiled. He snapped his fingers again. When I woke up the second time, he was gone. Nobody was around. I watched them row back to the ship. Peter was with them," Wendy finished, keeping her eyes training on Captain Hook. He had stopped swinging his sword and was staring intently at the back of her head. He shoved his sword into its sheath at his hip.

"How does he move around this island so swiftly?" Captain Hook muttered, stroking his beard. Wendy shrugged, then realized he wasn't looking at her. She remained silent, glancing at the cabin doors. Captain Hook turned around, muttering to himself. Wendy took the opportunity and jumped out of the chair. She grabbed the sword off the desk as she moved around it. She sprinted toward the doors, throwing them open and racing into the thick of the fighting. She realized there were considerably fewer boys fighting off pirates than before. The pirates were starting to win.

"What do we do, Wendy?" Jim cried, doing his best to fight off two pirates at once. Wendy spun in a circle, panic creeping up her chest and into her throat. Her heart started beating quickly and she tried to catch her breath. She didn't know what they should do. She didn't know why she was in this situation. She didn't know what to say.

10

"*P*oor, sad, scared, alone Wendy. Whatever will you do? Who will protect you? Who will protect them? What happens now?" Captain Hook taunted as he stepped through the doorway of the cabin. He smiled a victorious and vicious smile. He grabbed his hat off his head and bowed low, the pirates on board the ship started to clap. Wendy narrowed her eyes at him.

"You may have bested some of these boys. You may have caused Peter to run off. You may have the upper hand, but I am telling you this now - you will not defeat me," Wendy declared. Captain Hook planted his hat back on his head and raised his eyebrows in surprise.

"My dear, Wendy, I believe I already have," Captain Hook responded. Wendy crossed her arms, the sword hanging near her side.

"I beg to differ," Wendy replied. Captain Hook glanced at the pirates nearest him. They all shrugged, looking just as confused as he did.

"What do you mean?" Captain Hook asked, narrowing his eyes at her.

"I still have my sword, don't I?" Wendy asked. Captain Hook nodded. She smiled. She whirled it around her body, bringing it to rest, pointing at Captain Hook. He raised an eyebrow.

"Well, then. Let's have us a good old-fashioned sword fight," Wendy replied. Captain Hook smiled, pulling his sword out and preparing for a fight. He lunged, swinging the sword over his head and straight down at Wendy's head. She threw her sword up, blocking his swing. She pushed him off and spun away. She raised her sword again, backing up slowly across the deck. All of the pirates and lost boys watched the fight. The ones Wendy got close to scampered out of the way. All eyes were on Captain Hook and Wendy.

"Cock-a-doodle-doo!" Peter's cry went out. All eyes raised to the mainmast, near the crow's nest, where Peter was standing proudly. He was holding onto a rope with a sword in his other hand.

"Peter?" Wendy asked, confused.

"It can't be!" Captain Hook growled. He turned back to Wendy, taking advantage of her being distracted. He swung his sword toward her and almost hit her, but something stopped him inches from her head. She turned to look at him, gasping in fear. She stumbled backward, away from his sword. He looked at what stopped him - Peter was standing next to him. Peter pushed Captain Hook's sword away and took a few steps to the side. Peter circled Captain Hook, his sword pointing straight at Captain Hook's chest.

"Nice of you to join us again, Peter," Captain Hook sneered. Peter smiled, bowing slightly at Captain Hook.

"It's my pleasure," Peter replied. Captain Hook swung at Peter, metal clanging together as the swords met in the air. Peter twirled around and blocked Captain Hook's sword again. Wendy watched as all of this happened, her mouth hanging open in confusion. She scrambled away as the fight got nearer to her. She made her way around the deck to stand near Tootles and Jim.

"How is this happening?" Wendy asked, her eyes locked on Peter and Captain Hook. They were stuck in a vicious battle, neither one looking like they were ever going to back down.

"What do you mean? Pirates raided our ship and now the captains are fighting," Tootles explained. He shrugged.

"B-but...how is he here right now? How did he get up on the mast? How did he get down here so quickly?" Wendy struggled to keep her voice level. Tootles shrugged again.

"He flew?" Tootles suggested. Wendy glanced at Jim, her surprise reflected on his face as well.

"I meant a real explanation," Wendy replied, crossing her arms and ducking as Captain Hook's sword swung over her head. Tootles ducked as well and turned toward her as he straightened up.

"That is a real explanation. Peter can fly," Tootles responded. Wendy scoffed.

"Fly? Like a bird or an airplane?" Wendy asked, sure Tootles was going to admit he was joking. He didn't. All he did was nod his head.

"B-but...that's impossible," Jim added. He looked in amazement at Peter, watching as Peter took a step and then leaped into the air.

"Oh!" Wendy gasped, her hand flying to her mouth.

"He's flying!" Jim exclaimed his hands on his head.

"Told you," Tootles muttered, shoving his hands in his pockets. All eyes were locked on Peter. He laughed, swinging his sword below him, narrowly missing Captain Hook.

"You stole my map, you swine!" Captain Hook bellowed.

Peter paused, flipping around so his head was near Captain Hook.

"Swine? That's not very nice, Captain. You shouldn't call people names," Peter mocked.

"Peter!" Wendy cried, reaching forward. Tootles grabbed her around her waist and held her back. Captain Hook swiped up at Peter's head, narrowly missing him again.

"You're so close, Captain, but so very far," Peter taunted him. He laughed as he spun around in the air doing cartwheels. He reached into his shirt, pulling out a tan scroll, waving it in Captain Hook's face.

"Is this what you want, Hooky? Come and get it!" Peter taunted him. He flew over to the helm, landing his feet lightly on the banister. Captain Hook growled, swinging his sword around. He slowly made his way up the staircase, each step purposeful.

"You can't escape me forever, Pan," Captain Hook snarled. Peter laughed.

"Old, cranky Captain Hook thinks he can defeat me! Peter Pan! What do you think, boys? Think he can do it?" Peter addressed the crew who were watching from the deck.

"No!" came the rallying cry from every lost boy. Wendy looked worried. Jim grabbed her hand and pulled her toward the stern. The pirates who had boarded their boat earlier were all focused on the confrontation happening in front of them.

"What are we doing?" Wendy hissed. Jim pulled her further back, moving slowly over to the side of the ship. He dropped her hand and peered over the edge.

"Jim?" Wendy asked, tapping his shoulder. He looked back over at her, a grim look on his face.

"We're getting out of here. Now," Jim said, pointing to the lifeboat that was tied on the side of the ship.

11

*W*endy's mouth dropped open as she realized what Jim was planning. She glanced back at everyone on the ship.

"We can't just leave!" Wendy hissed. Jim barely paid attention to her. He was grabbing some rope and tying it to the side of the ship. Wendy grabbed his arm, forcing him to pay attention to her.

"Did you hear me? We can't just leave, Jim," Wendy repeated. Jim scoffed.

"Why not?"

"They need our help. These pirates will take over the ship. They need everyone to help," Wendy argued. She let go of Jim's arm and crossed her arms.

"Wendy, Peter is going to kill you. Nobody on this ship cares about us. They're all lunatics. They don't care if someone dies. We need to get out of here. Now," Jim pleaded. Wendy stared at him, realizing how desperate and panicked he sounded.

"I'm not going, Jim. These boys have done a lot to make

sure we're taken care of and safe. I'm not about to abandon them," Wendy argued. Jim narrowed his eyes.

"You don't have much of a choice," Jim replied. He grabbed Wendy's arms and pulled her closer to the edge of the ship. She screamed, wiggling as much as she could to get out of his grip. He grunted as he pushed Wendy closer to the edge.

"I don't think you want to be doing that," Tootles said, tapping Jim on the shoulder. Jim and Wendy paused. They both looked at Tootles.

"Stay out of this," Jim growled.

"I don't think I will," Tootles replied, putting a hand on Jim's shoulder and pulling him away from the edge of the ship. Wendy slipped from Jim's grasp and fell to the deck. She grunted in pain, then scrambled up.

"Don't put yourself in the middle of this, Tootles. We're going to leave," Jim stated. He picked himself up off the deck and squared up to Tootles. Tootles didn't react to Jim's proclamation. He merely stood there, as if he was waiting. Jim growled, pulling his sword from his sheath and running at Tootles.

"Jim, knock it off!" Wendy cried. She started to run after him but felt a hand on her arm. She turned and saw Nibs was standing there. He was focused on Tootles and Jim, not paying much attention to her.

"Let Tootles get him squared away. We need to get the pirates off this ship before the real fight is over. Otherwise, we're done for," Nibs explained, jerking his head toward Peter and Captain Hook. Wendy looked over his head at the fight.

Captain Hook was panting, his hair covered in sweat. Even his feather was droopy. Peter, on the other hand, looked as spry as ever. He was laughing and flying around Captain Hook's head. He taunted Captain Hook, barely getting within reach and then easily jumping out of the way again.

"How long do these fights usually last?" Wendy asked out of the side of her mouth. Nibs shrugged.

"Sometimes it can go on for hours and sometimes it's really quick. You never really can tell. It depends on how angry Captain Hook is that day. He usually blames all of his bad luck on Peter, so it depends on how badly his day has gone," Nibs replied. Wendy frowned.

"How often does this happen?" Wendy asked. Nibs shrugged again.

"I'd say, pretty much every day," Nibs replied. Wendy scoffed, shock rendering her speechless.

"Every day? How do you get anything done?" Wendy asked. Nibs frowned.

"What do you mean?"

"Well, you spend your entire day fighting with pirates. When do you have time to do anything else?"

"What else would we do?"

"I don't know...explore the world? Meet new people? Keep the ship clean? Go on adventures?" Wendy threw her hands up. She couldn't believe what she was hearing. Nibs frowned, shrugging.

"This is the adventure. We sail to Skull Rock, we raid the pirates' camp, we steal their treasure map and take their treasure. That's what we do," Nibs responded.

"How does the treasure get back each night?"

"What do you mean?"

"I mean, if you end up stealing the treasure and the map every day, what happens to make it go back to where you found it? If you end up taking it every day, how does it get back to where it was?" Wendy clarified, taking a step back and leaning back as Captain Hook's sword swung wildly in her direction. Nibs frowned, thinking over what she asked.

"I...don't really know. We never really asked. All we know is that we wake up, we go after the treasure map, and then get the treasure. Honestly, this is the first time things haven't gone like they always do," Nibs responded.

"And why do you think that is?" Wendy asked. She was trying to wrap her head around living the same day over and over. It would drive her mad being stuck doing the same thing day in and day out.

"Honestly? It's probably because of you," Nibs responded. Wendy watched as the twins knocked a couple of pirates over the head and threw them onto their ship, which was still anchored to Peter's ship.

"Jim and me?" Wendy clarified. Nibs shook his head.

"Nope. If it was just Jim, I think everything would still be the same. I don't think things would have changed. *You* changed them, Wendy. You're the one who changed the rules," Nibs responded. Wendy raised her eyebrows in surprise.

"Me?" Wendy asked, mostly to herself. Nibs nodded anyway. Wendy looked over at Peter, her stomach doing quick backflips. She couldn't help the smile that came to her lips while watching him, as much as she tried to hold it back. She was vaguely aware that Nibs knocked out a pirate beside her. He motioned for a few of the boys to help him. They hauled the pirate to the other side of the ship and tossed him back where he belonged. Wendy's eyes were locked on Peter.

She watched the way he flew through the air, laughing and carefree. She watched as he swung his sword and poked at Captain Hook, no fear in his face at all. She stared at his face, noticing his cute dimples and the way his eyes shone playfully as he fought.

"Uh...Wendy?" Nibs interrupted her thoughts. She shook her head, turning her focus to him.

"Yeah?"

"We should probably get moving now. Things are going to get really chaotic in a few minutes," Nibs explained, glancing at Peter and Captain Hook. The good Captain was slowing his swinging sword, his stream of insults and threats having long since extinguished. Wendy nodded, turning to check in with Tootles and Jim.

Jim was wildly swinging at Tootles, while Tootles stood there, ducking around every blow Jim attempted to deliver. Tootles was calm and patient, his sword not even drawn. Jim was panting, sweat starting to run down his face. His teeth were bared and he had a wild look in his eye.

"What are you going to do with Jim?" Wendy asked Nibs. He shrugged, watching Tootles and Jim.

"Tootles will probably have him put in the brig for a few hours. We can't really keep anyone in there forever," Nibs explained.

"Why not?"

"Tootles said we can't," Nibs offered as an explanation. Too Small was running by them and Nibs called him over.

"Get me the twins, will you?" Nibs asked Too Small. He nodded and ran to the other side of the ship, weaving and ducking his way through pirates who were resisting the boys' attempt to get them back on their ship. He made it to where the twins were heaving pirates over the edge onto their own ship. A pile of unconscious pirates was at their feet.

"Hey, Twins! Nibs wants you," Too Small called out. The

twins glanced at each other, then grinned. They turned around, scanning the boys closest to them.

"Curly, Slightly, come take over, will you?" One of the twins called out. Curly was an overweight boy who had light brown hair. He almost looked like a beach ball. If Curly was a large boy, Slightly was the exact opposite. He was tall and skinny, reminding Wendy of a twig. The boys glanced at each other and grumbled as they walked over.

"How come we gotta do this?" Slightly whined. His voice was high-pitched and made Wendy's ears hurt. She cringed a little bit, wondering how Peter had been okay with listening to him.

"Yeah, how come we gotta do this? Why aren't you two doing it? Peter said it was your turn," Curly agreed. His voice was deeper, but not by much. The twins sighed at the same time.

"Too Small was sent here to get us. Nibs wants us," The other twin explained. Curly and Slightly both groaned, kicking at the deck.

"That's not fair! You can't be getting out of your duties," Curly said.

"Yeah, you need to do your job. We shouldn't have to do it for you," Slightly added.

"Nibs needs us. What do you want us to do?" One of the twins asked. Curly and Slightly glanced at each other. They shrugged, not having any other option to add.

"We don't know," Slightly offered. The twins glanced at each other and then shrugged at Curly and Slightly. They walked away without adding anything else. Curly and Slightly got into the positions the twins had just vacated. They started picking up and moving pirates over to the other ship.

"Hiya, Nibs! What did you want us for?" One of the twins asked, walking over to where Nibs and Wendy stood.

"Hey, twins. We need your help getting Jim to the brig," Nibs explained. The twins glanced at Jim and nodded, not asking any clarifying questions. They walked over to where Jim was still wildly swinging at Tootles. They waited until he had made a big swing, knocking himself mostly off-balance. They latched onto his arms and got him under control. They then started dragging him down the stairs. Wendy watched all of this in silence.

12

"Thank you, Nibs," Tootles said as he walked over to where Wendy and Nibs were standing. Nibs nodded and then walked away. He started pointing out different things that the lost boys needed to do or avoid. Wendy looked at Tootles.

"Thank you for saving me," She said, shifting her weight uncomfortably. Tootles merely stared at her.

"I prevented him from running off with one of our shipmates. It was what I would have done for any crew member here. There is no need to thank me," Tootles replied. His voice was monotone, with no real emotion coming out.

"I'm part of the crew?" Wendy asked, raising her eyebrows. Tootles nodded.

"Of course. You became part of the crew as soon as you stepped onto the ship," Tootles responded. Wendy frowned at hearing that.

"So everyone who steps onto the ship becomes part of the crew? What about all of the pirates who come on board, trying to take over?" Wendy asked. Tootles cracked a small smile.

"Ah, you've got me there. They are not part of the crew, but yes, if you are not a pirate, then as soon as you step onto the deck, you become part of the crew. That's how it works around here," Tootles shrugged, starting to walk away. Wendy caught his arm, causing him to turn and look at her. She was frowning and had worry written all over her face.

"What happens if I don't want to be part of the crew anymore?" Wendy asked, not sure she really wanted to know the answer. Tootles' face darkened and Wendy was sure she didn't want to know the answer. She needed to know anyway.

"Nobody leaves the ship," Tootles responded. He pulled away from Wendy's grasp and continued on his way. He ordered a few of the lost boys to start working on repairs. Wendy was too stunned to try to stop him. Her mind was reeling from what Tootles had just told her. She had no doubt in her mind that what he said was true. The tone in his voice told her that. What she didn't know is what exactly that meant or how it worked for her, since she was a girl. She gulped.

Wendy walked along the deck, trying to quiet her mind. She heard the sounds of everything going on aboard the ship as if they were far away. She turned as Peter came flying up to her. He had a large grin on his face. He shoved his sword in his sheath and straightened his shirt.

"Wasn't that an awesome adventure?" Peter asked. Wendy hesitated. Peter's smile faded.

"What?" Peter asked.

"Well, it's something Tootles said," Wendy responded. Peter frowned, glancing over at Tootles.

"What did Tootles say?"

"He said that nobody leaves the ship," Wendy said. Peter's frown deepened.

"Why would you want to leave the ship?"

"Because you don't want a girl on the ship. That's what you said, isn't it? And I don't want you to be upset," Wendy reasoned. She tried to be as nonchalant as possible, but Peter still narrowed his eyes at her. She shrugged.

"It was just something I was confused about. Anyway, what happened to Captain Hook?" Wendy asked, looking around the deck. Most of the pirates were gone. Captain Hook's ship was still next to theirs, looking abandoned. There was no sign of life anywhere.

"The boys put him on his ship," Peter shrugged. He walked up the stairs to the helm. He stood at the banister, planting his hands on his hips. He smiled as he surveyed everything that was happening.

"What do you mean? You didn't kill him, did you?" Wendy asked, following Peter. Her face was full of alarm. Peter scoffed.

"No," He replied. Wendy eyed him closely. His face grew red and he turned away.

"Tell me the truth, Peter," Wendy pushed him. Peter cleared his throat. He watched as Tootles climbed the stairs toward them.

"Captain. Wendy," Tootles greeted them, giving them both a nod. Peter nodded back. Wendy offered Tootles a tentative smile. She still wasn't sure how she felt about Tootles after their last talk.

"Where to, Peter?" Tootles asked, taking his station at the helm. Peter glanced behind him, thinking.

"I think we should head straight for the treasure," Peter mused. Tootles nodded, not needing anything else from him. He turned the wheel and started steering away from Captain Hook's ship. Wendy stepped closer to Peter.

"Peter, did you kill Captain Hook?" Wendy asked again.

Peter looked at her, sideways. A small smile made its way across his face. Wendy pulled back, horror crossing her face.

"Peter never kills Captain Hook. He puts him back on his ship and sails away. That's how it's always done," Tootles answered her. She couldn't tear her gaze away from Peter's face.

"Nothing else has gone how it normally goes, has it, Tootles?" She responded, not bothering to look at him. He didn't have an answer for her. Wendy backed away, walking down the stairs. She wrapped her arms around her waist, rubbing one of her arms unconsciously. She found herself wondering if she should have gone with Jim when she had the chance.

"Hey, Wendy. Can you come over here real quick?" Too Small called out to her. She walked over to him, her arms still wrapped around her. She ruffled his hair when she got closer, enjoying the chestnut color of it. He scowled, but then giggled as she did it.

"What's up, Too Small?" Wendy asked. Too Small looked a little embarrassed. Slightly came walking up behind him.

"Come on, Too Small, ask her," Slightly urged him. Wendy waited patiently for Too Small to work up his courage.

"Wendy, would you read us a bedtime story?" Too Small pleaded. His voice rose an octave as he asked. Wendy was surprised, but she smiled warmly.

"Why, of course, I will. I'd love to," She replied. The boys all cheered, smiling and patting Too Small on the back. They dispersed and went back to their positions.

"Wendy," Peter called out. Wendy stiffened. She turned around and watched as Peter descended the stairs and walked over to her. She cleared her throat, glancing down at her feet as she shifted her weight uncomfortably. Peter stopped a few feet from her, glancing over at Too Small, who was still standing next to her. He squeaked and scampered off to whatever job he was supposed to be doing. Peter turned his attention back to Wendy.

"Wendy?" Peter asked again. Wendy fixed her gaze on him, attempting to force her heart rate back to normal.

"Yes?" She asked, doing her best to keep her voice steady. Peter raised an eyebrow.

"Can I show you something?" Peter asked. Wendy glanced around, hoping to find some type of excuse so she didn't have to be alone with him. Seeing nothing, she sighed.

"Alright," She replied. Peter grinned and took her hand. Wendy glanced over his shoulder at Tootles, who had a serious look on his face. It didn't make Wendy feel any better. Peter pulled her toward the stern. He glanced over his shoulder, making sure nobody was watching them. He reached up and grabbed a rope that was attached to one of the masts near them. He wrapped an arm around Wendy's waist and pulled her closer to him. Her stomach flipped at the closeness of him.

"Oh!" Wendy exclaimed as she was pulled upward. She looked down, realizing the deck of the ship was quickly fading away. She grabbed tightly onto Peter, worried about falling. She heard him laugh, a sweet, soft laugh that tickled her ear and made her stomach do more flips that had nothing to do with the sensation of flying. She cleared her throat, looking up at him. He was focused on her, not paying attention to where the rope was swinging. Her eyes widened as she realized they were heading straight for the largest mast on the ship.

"Peter!" She exclaimed in worry. Peter laughed again, closing his eyes and throwing his head back. He wrapped his hand around the rope and yanked, forcing the rope - and their bodies - to change directions. This time, they were flying straight up to the sky. The rope swung them around the yardarm a few times, tying up a sail. Peter let go of the rope as they fell, helping them land softly on the yardarm. Wendy let loose a relieved breath.

"Were you worried?" Peter asked, his voice soft. She looked up into his eyes. She realized they were still very close to each other. She took a step back, trying to put some distance between them. She stumbled on the thin surface. Peter reached out and steadied her, keeping his hand on her shoulder.

"Um...no. Of course not," Wendy stuttered. Peter's eyes twinkled as he smiled. Wendy found herself smiling back without even thinking about it.

13

"Um...what did you want to show me?" Wendy asked, clearing her throat again. She looked away, silently cursing herself for getting swept up in Peter's influence. She tried reminding herself that he probably killed Captain Hook - and countless others - and that she shouldn't be letting herself get swept up in his charisma. He was probably going to kill her too.

"Yes! Look that way," Peter grinned. He pointed behind her. He kept a hand on her waist as she slowly turned around on the balance beam they were standing on fifty feet into the air. Her breath came in a series of pants as she stared at the deck that was way too far away for her taste. Peter chuckled in her ear, his hot breath blowing over her neck. Goosebumps trickled down her arms and back.

"There...you see it?" Peter whispered. He drew close, pulling her to lean against his chest. She struggled to keep her mind clear, acutely aware of where her body was placed, and how unflattering the parts she hated were.

"See what?" Wendy replied, her voice breathless. Peter touched her chin gently.

"Look and see..."

She looked up, noticing the sun was sinking below the horizon. The sky was ablaze with a bunch of colors. The sea was reflecting everything the sky created. It was a beautiful melody that two parts of nature danced to and created together. It might not seem like these two parts would ever work together, especially with both parts affecting each other. The relationship they were creating with the sun as their bridge took Wendy's breath away.

"There. You see it, don't you?" Peter whispered. Wendy nodded, unfallen tears in her eyes. Peter smiled - a small smile that didn't have any games behind. There was no pretending. This was one of Peter's first real smiles in a long time. He couldn't even remember when he had smiled like this. He was glad Wendy couldn't see him.

"Oh, Peter. It's so beautiful," Wendy breathed. She was so moved by how beautiful everything looked. She completely put the distasteful business with Captain Hook out of her head. She watched as the sun sank below the horizon, lighting the entire sky on fire. The tears that sat in her eyes finally trickled down her face and pooled under her chin. Peter gently brushed them away. Wendy turned to look at him.

"Thank you for sharing this with me, Peter," Wendy whispered. She gave him a peck on the cheek. He pulled away in surprise and she threw her hands out, trying to catch her balance. Peter raised a hand to his cheek, oblivious to the fact that Wendy was struggling. Wendy screamed as she fell off the yardarm, plummeting straight to the deck. Peter blinked, realizing she wasn't standing in front of him anymore.

"Oh," Peter said, glancing down. He jumped off the

yardarm, reaching a hand down. He grabbed onto Wendy's hand inches before she hit the deck. She gasped in surprise. He gently lowered her all the way to deck. The lost boys gathered around her, all of them asking if she was okay. Wendy took a few deep breaths, not able to calm down her heart rate. She was hit with a complete feeling of over-whelm. She struggled to get away from everyone, stumbling as she made her way across the deck.

"Wendy?" Peter asked, his face looking puzzled. Wendy glanced over at him.

"He doesn't know why you're acting like this," Tootles offered as a way of explanation. Wendy jumped, surprised to find him at her side. She looked between Tootles and Peter. Her brain was still trying to process everything and once she had caught up, she started to laugh. It wasn't one of those normal laughs. It was a hysterical laugh. A reaction to almost dying. It puzzled Peter even more. He looked at Tootles in concern. Tootles just stood there, watching Wendy laugh.

"What is going on?" Peter said, frowning. He was getting impatient with Wendy's odd reaction.

"This is a normal reaction to almost dying, Peter," Tootles explained, still watching Wendy. Peter crossed his arms, scoffing.

"But she didn't die. I saved her," Peter responded. Tootles rolled his eyes but made sure Peter didn't see.

"Let her get it out of her system. Once it's gone, she'll need to be taken care of," Tootles responded. Peter threw his hands up and scoffed.

"This is why girls shouldn't be on pirate ships. They never like adventure," Peter whined. He pushed off the deck and flew up to the crow's nest. He crossed his arms and stared out at the fading twilight, pouting. Tootles glanced up, sighing. He wrapped his arms around Wendy's laughing frame and steered her into the captain's cabin. The laughter was starting to fade. She started sucking in deep breaths. The lost boys watched all of this happen, staring at Wendy as she was steered into the cabin.

"Back to work, the lot of ya," Tootles snapped over his shoulder. The boys jerked and ran back to their positions. Tootles opened the cabin door and steered Wendy inside. He sat her on the edge of the bed and walked back to the doorway.

"Too Small! Get me a cold rag and a cup of freshwater," Tootles called out of the door. He shut the door behind him, walking over to where Wendy sat. He grabbed her hand and patted it softly.

"It'll be alright, Wendy. I know you're in shock right now, but you'll be alright. We just need to ride this out," Tootles muttered to her. Too Small burst in, carrying a rag that was dripping wet and a glass cup of water. He stood just inside the doorway, staring at Wendy. Tootles glanced behind him, noticing Too Small was staring. He let go of Wendy's hands, stood up, and grabbed the stuff from Too Small's hands. He shoved Too Small out of the room and slammed the door shut with his foot. He walked over to where Wendy sat and placed the cup on the floor. He rang the rag all over the floor and then placed it on the bed next to her. He grabbed the cup and helped her take a small sip.

"Alright, let's lie back for a bit," Tootles muttered. He helped her lie back on the bed, putting the cold rag on her forehead. He stood back up and sighed, putting his hands on his hips. He stared down at her, shaking his head.

"Just rest for a bit. Hopefully, you'll feel back to normal

soon," Tootles said. He backed out of the room, closing the door quietly. Wendy stared up at the ceiling, not saying or doing anything - not even when the water dripped down her head and soaked her back.

14

"Wendy? Where are you?" Peter burst into the room. The doors slammed against the wall, making Wendy jump. She still didn't move. Her gaze was still trained on the ceiling. Peter marched over to where she was laying.

"Wendy? What are you doing lying down? We're supposed to be having an adventure!" Peter exclaimed. He jumped up on the bed, staring down at Wendy. Her eyes flicked toward him and then went back to the ceiling. Peter frowned. He jumped down to his knees.

"Wendy?"

"Not now, Peter," Wendy replied, her voice cracking. Peter crossed his arms.

"This is not an adventure," Peter responded. Wendy sighed heavily, pushing herself up on her elbows. She looked at Peter, annoyed at his insistence to play. She sighed again, pushing herself into a seated position.

"Peter, I don't want to have an adventure," Wendy said.

"What? Of course, you do! It's so much fun!" Peter argued. Wendy frowned.

"No, Peter. I don't. I want to lie here and think about how I almost died," Wendy argued. Peter scoffed.

"You didn't die. I saved you," Peter snapped. It was Wendy's turn to scoff.

"Something did happen! I was an inch away from dying! Just because you saved me doesn't mean that it didn't happen," Wendy rolled her eyes.

"You're fine. You're making a big deal out of nothing."

"Peter, when someone almost dies, it leaves a mark. It takes a toll on that person. It's not something most people can brush off and move on with their life. It takes a little while for a person's mind to come to terms with the fact that their life could have ended," Wendy explained. Peter opened his mouth to argue but closed it instead. He thought about what she said. He huffed and pushed off the bed. He crossed his arms as he stared out at the ocean.

"So does this mean you don't want to play anymore?" Peter pouted. Wendy chuckled softly.

"Did you kill Captain Hook?" Wendy asked. Peter scowled.

"Why is that such a big deal for you?" Peter pouted. Wendy raised an eyebrow. Peter scowled again.

"Fine, no, I didn't kill him. Are you happy?" Peter snarled. Wendy smiled smugly.

"Yes, I am," She replied, inching her way to the edge of the bed. She stood up slowly. Peter backed up and watched her stretch.

"Alright, Peter. You win. We'll have an adventure, but we're doing it my way," Wendy replied. She turned toward him, raising an eyebrow. Peter looked unsure but nodded.

"Okay...I'm not sure a girl can pick a good adventure, but I'll go with it," Peter replied. Wendy crossed her arms and smirked.

"You'd be surprised."

"I don't think I will be, but let's do this," Peter smiled. He clapped his hands and led the way out of the cabin.

"Lads! We're going to have an adventure," Peter yelled at everyone. Wendy thought she heard a few of the boys groan, but couldn't be sure. She followed slowly behind him and emerged from the cabin.

"What kind of adventure are we talking about here?" Tootles asked as he descended the staircase. Wendy glanced in his direction. He raised an eyebrow at her. Peter clapped his hands again, laughing and twirling around the deck, a few feet off the ground.

"We're going to go on a Wendy adventure!" Peter clapped.

"A Wendy adventure?" Tootles looked at her. She felt her cheeks grow warm and ducked her head to avoid his stare.

"Wendy? Care to elaborate?" Peter smiled. He seemed oblivious of Tootles' stare. He was excited about the adventure they were going to go on. Wendy cleared her throat, doing her best to ignore Tootles. She turned to the rest of the crew.

"Alright, well, for this adventure, there are several things we're going to need. First is going to be Captain Hook's treasure. We will also need a jug of rum, a brand from the Trading Company, and a special chalice that was said to have been used by the most infamous pirate of all - Francis Drake." Wendy instructed everyone. They all glanced at each other in confusion.

"That's no fun. Why would we want to find a bunch of things? It's like a bunch of chores. I don't want to do that," Peter crossed his arms, frowning. Wendy sighed and rolled her eyes.

"It's not like chores. It's like...a treasure hunt. You have to find these things to be able to move to the next part of the adventure. It's like a puzzle," Wendy explained. Peter's face brightened and he released his arms. He smiled, clapping his hands again.

"Ooo, it's like a game! I love games," Peter said. He skipped around the deck, dancing with a few of the younger boys. They laughed as they danced with him. The older boys looked unsure. They glanced around, stepping away from Peter as he came near them.

"Where do we start?" Tootles asked, taking a step forward. Peter finished skipping and came to stand near Wendy. She shifted her weight, uncomfortable to be so near to both of them.

"Well, we already have Captain Hook's map. Let's start by getting Captain Hook's treasure," Wendy suggested. Peter crowed. Tootles nodded.

"Heading north northwest, lads! Heave! Ho!" Tootles called, as he made his way back up to the stairs to the helm. Wendy let loose a breath. Her body felt exhausted and all she wanted to do was go to sleep. She sighed, rubbing her eyes.

"Wendy?"

Wendy put her hands down and blinked, seeing Too Small standing in front of her. Her eyebrows raised and she smiled. She bent down to his eye level.

"How's it going, Too Small?" Wendy asked.

"You promised to read us a bedtime story..." Too Small said. Wendy's smile widened.

"That I did. Is it time already?" Wendy asked. Too Small nodded, then ducked his head. Wendy ruffled his hair.

"Then, let's get going," Wendy said, wrapping her arm around Too Small's shoulders and steering him toward the crew quarters. They walked down the stairs together and into the crew's living quarters. Wendy looked around, noticing how dark and dank the area was. There were hammocks spread in two rows with boxes and barrels stacked all along the walls. Sacks of clothes were thrown hazardously around the room. A few of the boys were swinging in their hammocks, playing with yo-yos or whittling pieces of wood. Too Small ran ahead, making his way nimbly over all of the stuff lying on the ground. Wendy picked her way slowly and settled on the hammock, wrapping Too Small in her arms.

"This story takes place in a marvelous land where little boys and girls could play all day. It had a magical garden where plants and flowers grew wildly, growing tall and stretching toward the sun. The garden was flooded with magical creatures that danced in the sunlight and lit up the sky at night. These creatures tended to the plants and flowers within the garden. They also cared for the little boys and girls, making sure they had enough food and games to play." Wendy started her story. All of the boys settled down and listened to Wendy tell her story.

Wendy told a magical tale of little boys and girls who played through the magical garden and danced all day. Her tale went on and on, the boys never interrupting her. They remained as still as boys could. Wendy finished her tale, reminding the boys to get some sleep. She kissed Too Small's head and helped him lay down in the hammock. She walked out of the quarters, doing her best to be as quiet as possible. She ascended the stairs and looked up at all the stars littering the sky.

15

"*T*hat was quite a story," Peter said. Wendy's head snapped toward him. He was sitting on the banister, overlooking the main deck. She smiled at him.

"Did you enjoy it?" Wendy asked. Peter nodded, going back to the piece of wood in his hand. He continued to whittle it down, trying to look nonchalant. Wendy's smile widened.

"What was your favorite part?" Wendy asked, crossing her arms. Peter smiled, swinging his other leg over the banister and floating down toward her. He pretended to think about it.

"I'd have to say, the part where the little boys and girls played games all day," Peter replied. Wendy laughed, throwing her head back and letting her entire body feel it.

"How very Peter of you."

"I didn't know you could tell stories like that. Why didn't you tell me before?" Peter sulked.

"Oh, Peter," Wendy sighed. She shook her head, a smile playing on her lips. She walked over to the side of the ship, staring out at the dark ocean. The wind played at her hair, pulling it behind her. Peter walked over and stood behind her.

"What?" He whispered. He moved closer. Wendy shivered.

"What do you want from me?"

"I want you," Peter responded. Wendy sighed, shaking her head again.

"I can't give you what you want, Peter."

"But you can. You're what I want."

"What happens when you get bored of me? What happens if I want to get off the ship? What do we do if we have a fight? This is a small ship, Peter. You can't always get what you want," Wendy asked, turning to face him. He was very near her now, his eyes staring straight into hers. She sucked in a breath, struck by how bright his blue eyes truly were in the dark.

"Wendy, we could be each other's adventure - forever. All you have to do is stay with me. Stay with me forever, Wendy," Peter urged her. Wendy leaned into him. She took in a deep breath and looked into his eyes.

"Peter, I want nothing more than to stay with you...but I can't," She whispered. Peter frowned, pulling back.

"What?"

"I can't stay with you, Peter," Wendy whispered. Peter stumbled back a few steps, his face conveying the betrayal he felt. Wendy sighed, dropping her head. She took a step forward, tryiing to lay a hand on Peter's arm.

"No!" Peter yelled. He stumbled back even farther.

"Peter, please!" Wendy cried.

"No!" Peter yelled again. He bent down and pushed off the deck, flying up into the dark night. Wendy sighed, losing sight of him almost immediately. She wiped a hand across her forehead, the exhaustion pulling at her again.

"Wendy?" Tootles called out. Wendy whipped around, panic pulling at her. She narrowed her eyes at him, not quite sure how to feel about him after the ominous statement he said a few hours earlier. He put his hands up, trying to convey he meant no harm. He walked closer to her.

"I come in peace," Tootles chuckled. He put his hands behind his back.

"What do you want?" Wendy asked, still not trusting him completely. Tootles looked up at the sky.

"It seems you have angered our Captain," Tootles remarked. Wendy eyed him. He didn't say that with any malice or anger. It was merely a statement. Wendy sighed, looking back out at the ocean.

"I did," She responded.

"What happened?"

"I told him something he didn't want to hear."

"Ah, that'll do it. He hates that more than not being able to have an adventure," Tootles sighed. Wendy shook her head.

"How do you deal with him?" Wendy asked.

"It does get taxing at times, but Peter has saved my life consistently. I wouldn't be where I am today without him. I put up with his attitude because he has given me so much."

"I can believe that. I've seen that side of him - very briefly. I wish I could see it more," Wendy responded. She turned back to Tootles with a sad smile.

"Give him time. It takes him a while to warm up to people - especially when it's someone who keeps telling him things he doesn't want to hear," Tootles shrugged. Wendy sighed, walking away from him.

"He likes you, you know?" Tootles called after her. She stopped and turned back to him.

"Seriously?"

"Yes. That's what's causing all of these changes. We've been stuck in a time loop, living the same day over and over, waiting for someone to break us out. Turns out - that someone is you," Tootles shrugged. He walked back up the stairs. Wendy watched as he walked, but he didn't turn back to her. She let loose a shaky breath, realizing her heart was pounding in her chest.

She walked over to the captain's cabin and pulled open one of the doors. She peered in, half expecting to see Peter sulking in a corner. When she realized it was empty, she walked all the way into the room. She closed the door behind her and walked over to the bed. She sank onto the edge, looking around the room. It was exactly the same but somehow looked completely different. It felt so empty without Peter's energy. She sighed again, moving to the front of the bed. She snuggled under the large blanket, sinking into the soft mattress.

"Cock-a-doodle-doo!" Peter crowed loudly. Wendy sat straight up in the bed with a gasp. Her heart was racing. She listened to the sounds that were bursting through the walls of the cabin. Feet stomped on the deck, shouts were heard from all of the boys, and a bell rang incessantly. She threw the blanket off of her, scrambling out of bed. She shoved her feet into the slippers on the floor and ran to the doors of the cabin. She threw one of them open and stepped into the doorway. She surveyed what was happening on deck.

"Move, Too Small!"

"Keep it going, Nibs!"

"Ouch, that was my foot, twin!"

"Peter's waiting! Hurry up!"

Wendy blinked, watching all of the boys try to get as close to Peter as they could.

"Well boys, we made it. We have finally found Captain Hook's treasure. Who's going to help me get it?" Peter asked. The lost boys all started shouting and jumping over each other to try to earn Peter's attention. Peter turned to his right and beamed.

"Tootles, it looks like you and I are going on another adventure!" Peter cried. Tootles gave Peter a tight smile but said nothing. Wendy frowned.

"What about me?" Wendy planted her hands on her hips and narrowed her eyes at Peter. Peter scuffed, rolling his eyes.

"What about you?" Peter replied. Wendy stomped over to Peter, stopping right in front of him.

"I want to go," Wendy said. Peter glanced at Tootles and then threw his head back and laughed.

"There is no way we're taking a girl out on this adventure. You'd mess everything up," Peter chuckled. Wendy raised her eyebrows and glanced at the lost boys crowded around her.

"Oh, I'm definitely going. You can't keep me here. Besides, if I don't go, there's no Wendy adventure." Wendy smirked. Peter scoffed, then frowned.

"That's not fair!"

"Is too."

"You're not coming with us!" Peter argued. He crossed his arms and stomped his foot. Wendy raised her eyebrows and crossed her arms too.

"Fine. Then we're not doing the Wendy adventure," Wendy responded. She turned on her heel and walked back to the cabin. She heard Peter scoff behind her.

"Tootles, make her do the adventure," Peter whined.

Tootles sighed and followed after Wendy. He opened the cabin door and walked in, closing the door behind him. Peter waited a few minutes before following them. He walked in to see Tootles leaning against the wall and Wendy sitting at the desk, with one leg slung over the chair arm.

"What's going on?"

ootles calmly looked at Peter but didn't say anything. Wendy glanced in his direction but didn't bother talking to him. Tootles and Wendy were discussing what knowledge Wendy had about the pirate captains and what she loved so much about them. Peter frowned.

"What are you doing?" Peter asked again. Tootles glanced over again, while Wendy sighed.

"We're having a conversation, Peter," Wendy responded. Peter frowned, looking at Tootles.

"You were supposed to make her do the adventure."

"No."

"What?" Peter blinked. Tootles stared at him, his face calm.

"I said, no."

"But...you do what I say."

"Peter, you need to let Wendy come along," Tootles responded. Peter blinked, glancing at Wendy. She looked smug. Peter frowned again.

"I told you I didn't want her to come," Peter responded. His voice started growing louder.

"I don't care. She's coming," Tootles responded. His voice was calm and steady.

"Fine! But she better keep up. I'm not waiting for her," Peter yelled, stomping out of the room. Wendy and Tootles grinned at each other. Wendy got off the chair and Tootles pushed off the wall. They walked out of the cabin. Peter and Wendy walked over to the lifeboat. Wendy got in, while Peter stood there with his arms crossed, pouting.

"Nibs, you're in charge until I get back. Slightly, don't let him do anything stupid. Too Small, you're in the crow's nest. Keep an eye on the horizon," Tootles was directing everyone. When he finished, he turned and dropped down into the lifeboat. The boat was lowered into the water. Wendy looked up at the ship. Peter was peering over the edge, staring at them.

"Isn't Peter coming with us?" Wendy asked, her eyes locked on Peter. Tootles grabbed the oars and started maneuvering them away from the ship.

"He is."

"How is he going to get there?" Wendy asked. She turned to Tootles, giving him a questioning look. Tootles stopped rowing to give her a pointed look.

"You realize he can fly, right?" Tootles asked. Wendy smacked her forehead with the palm of her hand.

"I completely forgot."

"You forgot that someone can fly?" Tootles asked, raising an eyebrow. Wendy shrugged.

"A lot has been happening," Wendy replied. Tootles grunted, not bothering to give a reply. He went back to rowing the boat. They made good time, rowing through the rough water. The shore came closer and Wendy scanned the beach. Her eyes roamed the island trees and rocks that lined up the edge of the beach.

"What is this place?" Wendy asked. Tootles glanced behind him, turning back to look at her.

"The locals call it The Jolly Roger," Tootles responded. Something about his tone sounded ominous to Wendy. She gulped, making the decision not to ask any more questions about the island. She steered the conversation in another direction.

"So, does Peter know where on the island Captain Hook hid his treasure?"

"Of course, we've found it many times. Captain Hook doesn't really do a good job hiding it."

"Does he put it in the same place every time? Like the map?" Wendy asked. Tootles nodded, his breath coming in pants from all the rowing he was doing. Wendy rolled her eyes.

"Captain Hook doesn't seem too bright. That surprises me - all the rumors about him paint him as a cunning and merciless pirate. They all end with the advice to never get in a fight with Captain Hook or it'll be the last thing you do," Wendy said. Tootles smirked.

"They aren't wrong."

"How can he be such a great fighter? He's not very intelligent from what I've heard," Wendy argued. She trailed a hand over the side of the boat, the cool water soothing her hot skin.

"I wouldn't do that if I were you," Tootles warned her. She looked over at him, her hand still in the water.

"Why not?" Wendy asked. She looked back in time to see something grab her wrist and pull her over the edge of the boat and into the water. Tootles set the oars down, sighing heavily. He rolled his eyes and stood up. He put his foot on the edge of the lifeboat and then dived into the water.

A few seconds passed by, a shadow crossing over the empty lifeboat. Tootles broke the surface of the water a few feet from the boat. He sucked in a deep breath. Wendy broke the surface right next to him, coughing and sputtering water out of her mouth. Tootles helped Wendy into the lifeboat and pulled himself into it. He gave an extra kick, hitting something that had started to snake around his ankle.

"That's why you don't put your hands in the water before you reach the shoreline," Tootles panted. He sat down and grabbed the oars. He started rowing again as if he hadn't just rescued Wendy.

"What was that?" Wendy yelled. She looked all around her, fear and panic starting to rise in her chest. She leaned over the edge to take a closer look. A face came roaring up to her, stopping just before it broke the surface. It was a beautiful woman, young and tan. Her long blonde hair flowed seamlessly with the ocean current. Her eyes were a bright blue and her lips were a luscious red. Wendy found herself leaning in closer. She heard a sweet melody, causing her body to relax.

"Back, demon!" Tootles yelled, slapping an oar over the woman's face. Wendy jerked back with a yelp. She stared at Tootles.

"What?" Tootles asked, raising an eyebrow. He sat back down and started rowing again.

"What are they?" Wendy asked, her voice light and airy. Tootles snorted.

"Mermaids," He spat. Wendy raised her eyebrows.

"Mermaids? Like real mermaids? With a tail and everything?" She asked. Tootles nodded. He didn't add anything to the conversation, so she huffed and sat back in the boat.

"Why are they here?" Wendy asked, leaning forward again, eyeing the water behind her. She was worried the mermaids would reach up and pull her into the water by her hair.

"What do you mean?"

"I mean what do they want? Why are they around this island?"

"Because of Peter," Tootles replied. He rowed into the shoreline and the waves started to tilt the boat. He expertly maneuvered it so it got closer to the shore. About ten feet from the beach, he jumped out and pulled the lifeboat up on shore. He held a hand out and helped Wendy get out of the boat.

"Thank you," Wendy replied. Her voice was small and restrained. She was nervous about being on this island. Everything about it screamed danger. It made her shiver in fear for no reason. She wanted to get back on the lifeboat and go back to the ship. She opened her mouth to tell Tootles that when Peter landed right in front of her. He plopped his hands on his hips and had a wide grin on his face.

"The mermaids almost got you!" Peter smiled. Wendy scowled, clamping her mouth shut. She wasn't going to let Peter be right. She was going to go on this adventure. She pushed past Peter and started walking down the beach.

"Where are you going?" Peter asked, following her. He skipped along next to her.

"I'm going to find Captain Hook's treasure," She responded. Peter laughed like it was something he found amusing. Wendy stopped and turned toward him. She planted her hands on her hips.

"Why is that funny?"

"Because, silly Wendy, you're going the wrong way! Plus, a girl getting Captain Hook's treasure before me? Never going to happen."

"Why don't we make a game out of it?" Wendy suggested. Peter eyed her suspiciously.

"What kind of game?" He asked.

"A race. To see who can get to the treasure first."

"Why would you want to race him? He can fly, remember? He's going to beat you in no time," Tootles called out. Peter grinned, looking triumphant. Wendy raised an eyebrow and smirked.

"Maybe, but we'll see," Wendy responded. Peter frowned, but seemed interested.

"Alright, here are the rules."

"Why do there have to be rules? Rules are not fun! I don't want to follow rules," Peter whined. Wendy sighed, running a hand down her face.

"Peter, rules are the only way to make the game fair," Wendy responded. Peter kicked at some shells in the sand, grumbling. Wendy rolled her eyes.

"Okay, here are the rules - Tootles and I get the map. You already know where the treasure is and the island as a whole. There's no flying allowed. The first one there is the winner," Wendy explained. Peter hopped from one foot to the other.

"Deal!" Peter yelled, excitement oozing out of his body. He pulled the map from behind him, handing it over to Tootles. He clapped his hands and smiled.

"Ready? Go!" Wendy shouted. Peter took off, running through the forest, not looking back. Wendy turned to Tootles.

"You know he's going to cheat. Why did you even play

this stupid game?" Tootles pouted. Wendy rolled her eyes and stuck out her hand.

"It will keep him preoccupied. Now, give me the map."

"No way! Why do you get to have the map?" Tootles argued, pulling the map away from her. Wendy frowned.

"Because it was my idea. Plus, I'm in charge." Wendy responded. Tootles laughed, throwing his head back. He grinned at her as he unrolled the map.

"No way are you in charge."

17

*W*endy followed behind Tootles, swatting at flies that buzzed near her head. Tootles kept muttering to himself, but she couldn't make out what he was saying. Wendy sighed for the millionth time as she swatted away the hoard of flies - for what felt like the millionth time.

"Are we almost there?" Wendy asked. Tootles didn't respond to her, so she tried again. She tapped his shoulder.

"Hey. Are we almost there?" Wendy repeated. Tootles came to a complete stop, causing Wendy to walk into his back. She scoffed and moved to his side.

"You didn't have to stop so abruptly just because you're annoyed. I only wanted to get an update," Wendy pouted. She opened her mouth to say more but closed it when she noticed Tootles' expression.

"What is it?" She asked, turning to look at what had startled him. She gasped, taking a step back. Tootles gripped her arm as a twig snapped under her foot. A ManyMore was right in front of them. It had long spiny black legs which lifted its fuzzy body. The pincers at the front of its face were as thick as Wendy's thigh. It chittered a searching sound. Tootles squeezed her arm so tightly it hurt, but Wendy hardly noticed. Her eyes traveled down, praying to not find Peter laying there. Underneath the ManyMore was a deer. She breathed a sigh of relief and then her eyes snapped back up to the creature.

"What do we do?" Wendy whimpered out of the side of her mouth.

"It's a cross between an ant, a spider, and some other creature we aren't too sure about. From what we can tell, it reacts to movement. So stay very still," Tootles responded in a low whisper. Wendy let loose a shaky breath. She closed her eyes as the ManyMore screeched. It reminded her of a cross between a dying dog and nails on the chalkboard. It made her shudder.

"Cook-a-doodle-doo!" Peter's cry sounded through the forest. The ManyMore reared up on its hind legs in response. Tootles sighed.

"This is not going to go well," Tootles muttered. Wendy looked sharply at him.

"Why do you say that?" She responded, keeping one eye on the ManyMore. It was chittering, starting to slowly walk around the area. It was making its way toward her.

"Peter loves to fight the ManyMore. You brought your sword, right?" Tootles asked. Wendy stiffened. She felt her side, realizing she had left the sword on the ship. She closed her eyes.

"No," She responded in a whisper. She dropped her hand, lowering her head. She felt a dagger being pressed in her hand. She opened her eyes and looked over at Tootles. His gaze was still locked on the ManyMore, but he responded to her questioning look anyway.

"You shouldn't be left defenseless. This will at least give you something to defend yourself with if it comes to it."

"If it comes to it?" She asked.

"When Peter breaks through, run for cover. Peter and I should be able to take it by ourselves. You shouldn't need to get involved."

"I'm not going to run for cover. I insisted on coming on this adventure. I'm going to pull my weight. Especially since you're away from Peter because of me," Wendy argued. Tootles sighed, slowly drawing his sword out of his sheath.

"Just watch its pincers and it's stinger."

"It's what?"

"The sharp things on its face and butt. They're both full of poison," Tootles explained. Wendy nodded.

"Got it," She responded. Peter burst through the trees behind the ManyMore, letting loose a loud cry. The Many-More screeched again, turning to face him. Tootles stepped forward and swiped at one of its legs. It went down with another scream. Thick green ooze started pouring out of the missing limb. Wendy covered her mouth and gagged. The smell was downright horrid.

Peter crowed again, pushing off the ground and doing a front flip over the ManyMore. He swung his sword as he flipped, cutting the ManyMore across it's back. It screeched again, this time in pain. Wendy started to feel bad, wanting to help the poor creature. That feeling went out the window when it lifted it's head and sent some white liquid flying toward her from its pincers. She screamed and leaped out of the way.

"Alright, let's kill this creepy bug!" Wendy yelled, getting to her feet. She lifted the dagger and charged, screaming as she did. Peter cheered her on, watching as she ran. She slipped down to one knee, sliding under the ManyMore.

The dagger ripped it's way across the ManyMore's stomach, more of the green ooze falling out, like a nasty waterfall. A long accordion thing, slightly pink and definitely bulged, fell out as well.

"Look, it's intestines!" Peter yelled, pointing at the ground. Wendy scampered out of the way, the ManyMore's ooze spreading closer to her. She didn't know if it would hurt her or not, but she didn't want to take the chance to find out. The ManyMore swayed on its legs, stepping all over its own intestines. It let out a final, painful screech and then thudded to the ground. The forest dived into silence, not even a bird daring to make a sound.

"That was incredible!" Peter yelled. Wendy jumped, surprised by the noise. She spared another nervous glance at the ManyMore, not quite sure it was actually dead. She made a wide berth around the body, walking over to where Peter and Tootles were standing. They were both staring at her with a look of awe on their faces.

"What?"

"How did you learn to do that?" Tootles asked. Wendy shrugged.

"I used to play softball. It was exactly like sliding into base. I just needed to make sure I hit the ManyMore and I was out of the way when whatever was in that thing came out," Wendy explained. Tootles stared at her. Peter wiped his sword on his sleeve and then put it back in its sheath.

"I'm impressed," Peter winked at her. She felt her cheeks growing hot and she bowed her head.

"We'd better get a move on. With all that screeching and noise coming from here, I'm sure more of the ManyMore's will be heading this way," Tootles interrupted. Wendy sighed, walking over to a nearby tree. She wiped the blade of her dagger off with one of it's huge leaves and shoved it into her belt. She turned around. Tootles was giving her a weird look.

"What?"

"Nothing. Let's go," Tootles responded, turning away. He shoved his sword, nasty bug ooze and all, into his sheath. He walked over and picked up the map that he had dropped when they first spotted the ManyMore. He rolled it up and tucked it into his waistband.

"Walk with me, Wendy," Peter said. Wendy looked at Tootles, who shrugged.

"Alright," Wendy responded. She and Peter led the way, walking next to each other. They talked the entire time they walked. Peter recounted the entire battle with the Many-More. Wendy thanked him for showing up when he did. Peter talked about the battles he had with the pirates and how he couldn't wait to get the treasure. Wendy asked who his favorite lost boy was.

Tootles walked behind them, keeping one ear on their conversation. He couldn't help listening to everything they said. He was supposed to be with Wendy - not Peter. They walked on for several minutes, Peter and Wendy chatting about everything under the sun. Tootles remaining silent and listening to every word.

"Peter, do you know where we're going?" Wendy suddenly asked, looking around. They were in the middle of the forest, trees surrounding them completely. Peter turned in a circle, searching the area. He frowned.

"Huh. No, I actually don't," He replied. Wendy looked worried. Tootles took a look around and then pulled the map out. He unrolled it and studied the markings.

"It looks like we need to head straight. Then, we'll find a stream. It'll take us to a cave, where the treasure is buried,"

Tootles instructed. Peter cheered, waving his hands above his head.

"Treasure!" He exclaimed. They set off, following the path. They all cheered and jumped around, excited to be close to the treasure.

18

*P*eter, Wendy, and Tootles walked for what seemed like forever. Wendy and Tootles had to convince Peter not to fly off several times. He had gotten bored and tired of walking. He ended up entertaining himself by running and scaring the birds and other wildlife they saw. He would climb trees and then float down to the ground while Wendy and Tootles tried to catch him.

"Are we there yet?" Peter whined for the millionth time. Tootles sighed, pushing back a tree branch. He paused, staring past the tree. He turned back to Peter with a smile on his face.

"Yes, Peter, we are," He said. He stepped aside and let Peter and Wendy look at what he had just found. It was a big opening in the middle of the forest. The area had a few big boulders around the edges, with bushes next to them. The cave was cut into the side of a rock wall, jagged edges surrounding the opening.

"Captain Hook's treasure! It's finally mine!" Peter laughed as he burst into the opening. Wendy followed, thanking Tootles for holding the branch for her. Tootles followed behind, his eyes sweeping the area. Peter ran to the opening of the cave, standing in the middle. He planted his hands on his hips and looked around the entrance.

"Tootles, is there anything on the map about what we need to do in the cave?" Wendy asked, turning to him. Tootles shook his head, staring at the map.

"Doesn't look like there's anything special," Tootles replied.

"Then, let's go!" Peter exclaimed, running forward. Wendy glanced back at Tootles, a worried look on her face. She sighed and followed Peter at a much slower pace.

"What's wrong?" Tootles asked, tucking the map away as he caught up with her. Wendy shook her head.

"I don't quite know. I feel like we're missing something. It feels like it was too easy," Wendy replied. She glanced behind her quickly when a sound echoed through the cave. Tootles chuckled.

"You spook easily," Tootles said. He patted Wendy's shoulder. She didn't respond. They walked in silence, Peter still running around and bouncing off the walls. The cave was dark and it wasn't long before they couldn't see around them clearly.

"Wendy! Tootles! You have got to see this!" Peter yelled from ahead of them. Wendy and Tootles stumbled their way around another corner, blinking in surprise at the sudden burst of light. They raised their hands to cover their eyes as they walked forward. They blinked a few times, their eyes adjusting.

"What is this place?" Wendy marveled, looking around the opening in the cave. There were diamonds and gems stuck in the walls. A pile of gold coins sat in a treasure chest on top of a hill. A pile of pearl necklaces was laying on the ground next to it. Golden crowns, coins, and other jewels were strewn all around the cave. A luscious waterfall near the back of the opening was churning water in a little stream throughout the opening. It was a beautiful, tranquil place.

"This is amazing," Tootles murmured. Peter was standing in the middle of the room, his gaze frozen on the chest in front of him.

"Peter?" Wendy asked, walking over to him. She glanced between him and the chest, a look of concern crossing her face.

"The treasure is mine," Peter muttered. Wendy gave him a small smile, patting his arm.

"Yes, it is, Peter," She responded. She turned away and spotted a large ruby laying on the ground. She bent over to pick it up but froze inches away from it.

"I've got you, at last, Peter Pan!" A voice cried out from the shadows. Wendy jerked her hand back and straightened up. She looked around her, shock and dread filling her body as she realized what was happening. Captain Hook and his men were entering the opening from hidden areas she hadn't noticed. Tootles backed up until he was at Peter's back. Wendy turned and put her back to them as well. She heard Tootles and Peter draw their swords.

"Come now. Surely you know when a fight has been lost, even before it has begun," Captain Hook tutted. He stepped into the opening further, his evil grin spreading wide across his face. Wendy recoiled at the sight of him.

He had cuts all over his face. His fancy hat had been stripped of its feather and lay limp on his head. His coat was ripped to shreds and his shoes had large holes in them. He walked with a limp. His long black curly hair was untamed and wild.

"What happened to you?" Wendy asked, the words

tumbling out of her mouth. She sensed a shift in the air, a tense feeling rippling through the pirates. They glanced uneasily at each other. She gulped, wanting to take the question back, but there was nothing she could do now.

"What happened to me, my dear, is your beloved Peter Pan!" Captain Hook yelled. His eyes were wide and had an unhinged look to them.

"How did Peter do this to you?" She challenged him. She crossed her arms.

"Peter taunted me until I was too weak to stand and then threw me in Crocodile Creek. I barely escaped with my life. That pesky crocodile already had one piece of me, thanks to that boy. It wants another!" Captain Hook screamed, flailing wildly. Wendy glanced at Peter, raising an eyebrow.

"Seems to me like you don't know when to cut your losses and stop the fight," Wendy countered. Tootles snickered. The pirates surrounding them laughed hesitantly. Captain Hook peered around, eyeing each one of them. They all fell silent.

"If I were you, I'd shut my mouth, girly. Otherwise, you won't like what will happen," Captain Hook threatened, shoving his hook in her face.

"Are we going to fight or are you going to stand there all day saying things nobody listens to?" Peter asked, pointing his sword in Captain Hook's direction. Captain Hook turned his attention toward Peter, a sly grin spreading across his face.

"Yes, of course. I wouldn't want to keep you waiting," Captain Hook said. He drew his sword out slowly, facing Peter. He took a step forward, causing Peter to take a step back. Tootles stepped out of Peter's way, his focus on the other pirates who were moving in. Wendy watched Captain Hook and Peter. Captain Hook took another few steps and

Peter stepped back in a similar fashion. Wendy was so engrossed in the fight, she almost missed the nasty trick Captain Hook was trying to play.

"Peter, look out!" Wendy cried. She pointed behind Peter, where a pirate was sneaking upon him with a bag, trying to throw it over his head. Peter ducked, sidestepping the pirate and laughed as he finally clashed swords with Captain Hook. The metal rang out, echoing in the cave.

Wendy was grabbed from behind, the pirates dragging her back. They pulled her hands behind her, but she stomped on the foot of the pirate holding her. He yelped and let go. She turned, whipping out the dagger from her waist. She jabbed at the two pirates standing in front of her. They backed away, whimpering as they jumped out of the range of her dagger. She rolled her eyes.

"Wendy, get over here!" Tootles snapped, swinging his sword at three pirates who were facing him. She glanced behind her, taking off toward Tootles. She stepped lightly, managing to miss most of the treasure that was lying on the ground. She heard the two pirates behind her attempt to go after her, but step into the treasure and thud to the ground. She laughed - she had never felt so alive.

19

"Why are you laughing?" Tootles asked, slashing down with his sword and then quickly standing up and blocking another sword heading his way. Wendy stopped next to one of the pirates who were in front of Tootles. The pirate stopped swinging his sword and looked at Wendy, the confusion plain on his face.

"Hi!" Wendy exclaimed. She plunged her dagger in the pirate's neck, pulling it out quickly. She took a step toward Tootles. The pirate slapped a hand to his neck, surprised at what happened. He stumbled, taking a step and coughing. The blood coming out of his neck spurted angrily toward the ground. The two pirates in front of Tootles glanced at each other and stared at Wendy in horror. She flashed them both a sweet smile, clasping her hands together and swinging her body side to side. The blood from the pirate's neck dripped off her hands, down onto the dagger, and hit the floor. The pirates turned on their heels and sprinted out of the cave. Tootles turned to Wendy.

"That was utterly terrifying."

"Thank you," Wendy responded, dropping into a small

curtsy. She grinned, wiping the dagger off. She stuck it into her waistband and turned around. Peter and Captain Hook were locked in an epic battle. The clanging of metal echoed in the cave. They were focused on the fight, not paying attention to the treasure they scattered around their feet. The coins made a clinking sound as they were scattered around the floor.

"What do we do about these two?" Wendy asked, planting her hands on her hips. Tootles shook his head. He shoved his sword in his sheath and sighed.

"I think it's time you gave Peter permission," Tootles responded.

"Permission for what?" Wendy asked, turning to Tootles. He gave her a long look and sighed.

"Permission to end Captain Hook," Tootles responded. Wendy blinked, surprised at his response. She looked back at the fight.

"Do you think he could really do it?" She muttered. Tootles scoffed and crossed his arms.

"Easily."

"Alright. How do I go about giving him permission?"

"Tell him to go for it. Tell him you want him to win the war, not just the battle," Tootles suggested. He jerked his head toward Peter and Captain Hook. Wendy sighed, still not sure what she was doing, but needed this to end once and for all. She took a few steps forward, careful not to get too close to the swords swinging wildly.

"Peter! Go for it! Win this war! Do what needs to be done so we can go home!" Wendy shouted. The sound echoed around the chamber. Peter and Captain Hook paused their fighting. Peter's eyes locked on Wendy and he smiled wildly. He nodded at her. Captain Hook looked around the cave, trying to figure out where the sound was coming from. His gaze landed on Peter, who was still looking at Wendy. Captain Hook glanced over his shoulder, glaring at Wendy. She gulped when she noticed his stare.

"I think you've done enough," Tootles suggested, gently pulling her back. She stumbled toward him, her gaze shifting back to Peter. He winked at her seconds before Captain Hook resumed swinging his sword. They went back to fighting, but Wendy noticed Peter wasn't playing anymore. He was making more strikes, using more force. There were more than a few nicks on Captain Hook's arms and legs from Peter's sword.

Captain Hook and Peter started making their way around the cave. The fight picked up speed and intensity. Captain Hook shouted in triumph when he finally nicked Peter's arm. Wendy gasped and took a step forward. Tootles put a hand on her to hold her back. Peter stared at the scratch on his arm, blood starting to pool ever so slightly. He looked up at Captain Hook, who was grinning broadly. Peter raised an eyebrow.

"End it, Peter!" Wendy shouted. Peter looked over at her and nodded. He blocked Captain Hook's incoming swing and ducked under the sword as it flew by where his face had been. He lunged, Captain Hook stumbling back quickly to miss the tip of the sword. Wendy frowned, watching the whole thing. She suddenly had an idea. She turned to Tootles with an excited look on her face.

"What?" He asked.

"I have an idea," She responded.

"Okay...tell me."

"Nope."

"What?"

"I'm not going to tell you. It's crazy and you're going to try to talk me out of it," Wendy responded, turning back to the fight. She watched as Captain Hook forced Peter around the treasure chest and back toward where she and Tootles stood. Tootles started backing up. Wendy stayed still. She put her arm behind her back, wrapping her hand around the dagger's handle. Peter came even closer. Wendy stepped to the side to let Peter come nearer. Peter stepped back right beside her. She grabbed his free hand, pulled the dagger from behind her back, and shoved it into his grip. Peter hesitated, clearly surprised at what was happening.

"I believe in you," Wendy whispered, staring straight into Peter's eyes. He stared at her, pausing the fighting. Captain Hook swung his sword down toward Peter's head. Wendy took a step back, her eyes still locked with Peter's. She smiled. He smiled, too. He brought his sword up, blocking Captain Hook's swing.

"Cock-a-doodle-doo!" Peter crowed. Captain Hook winced. Peter threw him off and started advancing. With a dagger in his free hand, Peter was gaining the upper hand. He nicked Captain Hook's arm again, then took a step forward and plunged the dagger straight into Captain Hook's neck. There was a moment of silence as the shock of what had happened sunk in for everyone in the cave. Peter took a step back, leaving the dagger in Captain Hook's neck. He was panting, staring at the dagger.

"Oh," Captain Hook strained, his hand roaming the dagger handle. He wheezed, taking in a deep breath. Then, he pulled the handle from his neck. Blood started spurting from the wound. He took a few staggering steps. He fell to his knees, dropping his sword. Peter grabbed it and circled him, watching as the life drained from his body. He toppled face-first into the dirt. Peter kicked at his shoulder lightly, making sure he really was dead.

"You did it," Tootles said, his voice sounding breathless

and disbelieving. Tootles looked at Peter, his eyes wide in shock. Peter didn't respond. He looked over at Wendy. She was already looking at him, a smile on her face and pride in her eyes.

"I did it," Peter said. She nodded slowly, taking careful steps around Captain Hook's body. She stepped closer until she was inches away from him.

"You did it," Wendy whispered. She pressed herself into Peter's chest, wrapping her arms around his body. He dropped both swords on the ground. They hardly made a sound as they hit the dirt. Peter wrapped his arms around Wendy, taking a deep breath. He breathed in her smell, a mix of the salty ocean air and a flowery smell. He released it, all the tension releasing from his shoulders.

"Let's get your treasure and go back to the ship," Wendy whispered. Peter nodded, not saying anything. He stepped out of Wendy's embrace and cleared his throat. He glanced over at Tootles, who was staring at them with his mouth wide open.

"Tootles, close your mouth before you get a fly in there," Wendy teased. She giggled. Peter shot her a wink and grinned.

"Tootles, come help me get our earnings out of this depressing cave," Peter instructed. Tootles shook his head, snapping out of his daze. He raised an eyebrow at Wendy but followed after Peter. Wendy gave him a mysterious smile but didn't say anything.

"To the ship!" Peter cheered. He grabbed one of the treasure chest handles and picked it up. Tootles followed suit. They slowly made it down the little hill and through the cave. Wendy picked her way around Captain Hook's body, grabbing a few pearl strands and wrapping them around her neck. She followed after Peter and Tootles, grabbing the swords Peter had dropped. They made their way out of the cave and to the clearing. Peter and Tootles set the treasure chest down, resting for a few moments.

"So, what happens now?" Tootles asked. Wendy handed a sword over to Peter. They both sheathed their swords.

"What do you mean?" Wendy asked. Tootles shrugged.

"Well, every day for as long as I can remember, we've sailed the seas, fought with the pirates, grabbed the map and the treasure, and then did it all over again the next day. Now that Captain Hook is dead and we have the treasure, what do we do now?" Tootles explained. Wendy and Tootles looked to Peter, who seemed to be deep in thought.

"I'm sure a new captain will be elected for the ship. We'll just have to play with them when the time comes," Peter responded, shrugging. Wendy smiled and slipped a hand around his waist.

"Besides, there are so many other adventures to explore outside of these waters," Wendy responded. Peter looked down at her in surprise. He opened his mouth to ask a question but was interrupted by a sound that stopped all life in the forest cold.

20

"Is that what I think it was?" Tootles asked, pulling his hands away from his ears. He gulped. Peter nodded, his face grim.

"I'm pretty sure that was. We need to get moving - now," Peter said, grabbing the handle of the treasure chest again. Tootles quickly moved into position and they started through the forest at a hurried pace. Wendy followed after them, her head on a swivel.

"Was that a ManyMore?" Wendy called out. She didn't hear any birds or feel any bugs flying around her head.

"No. That was *all* of the ManyMore," Peter responded over his shoulder. Wendy's blood ran cold. She looked all around her, not sure how to respond.

"We don't have much time, Peter," Tootles called out, panting. Peter didn't answer, only increased his speed. A crashing noise came through the forest on their left. Peter and Tootles jumped off the trail, ducking behind some trees. Wendy stopped and stared in the direction the noise was coming from. Tootles reached over and pulled her behind the trees just as a ManyMore three times the size of the one they had seen before burst onto the trail. It screeched again, causing Peter, Tootles, and Wendy to cover their ears.

"That's the queen," Peter whispered. He stared up at the eyes of the creature.

"What do we do?" Wendy hissed. Both Peter and Tootles shushed her. She hunkered back down, trying to catch a glimpse of the queen's head. The queen turned in both directions of the trail, as if she was trying to decide which way to head. She finally turned in the direction they had come from. She started crashing her way up the trail. Peter watched her go and then rose up. He turned to Tootles and Wendy.

"We have to go. If the queen is out of the safety of the nest, that means that thousands of ManyMore's are currently combing this island," Peter said. He sighed, looking down at the treasure chest.

"So, what do we do?" Tootles responded, his jaw set firmly. Peter shook his head.

"I don't know," He responded. Wendy glanced at the retreating ManyMore's back.

"Let's do this - Peter, can you carry the treasure chest by yourself?" Wendy asked. Peter raised an eyebrow but shrugged.

"Probably. As long as I get help getting a good grip on it," He responded. Wendy nodded.

"Alright, then you fly the chest back to the lifeboat. Tootles and I will make our way there on foot. Once you get the chest in the lifeboat, come back and help us get the rest of the way there. That way, we won't have to worry about the chest weighing us down. We can move faster and be free to fight if it comes to that," Wendy instructed. Peter glanced at Tootles, who shrugged.

"Sounds like a good plan to me," Tootles suggested. Peter shrugged.

"Alright. Let's do it," Peter responded.

"Crouch down," Wendy instructed Peter. He did what she told him. Wendy moved to the other side of the treasure chest and gripped the handle.

"Hands above your head, Peter. Ready, Tootles?" Wendy asked. Tootles grabbed the handle and nodded at her. She counted down and they swung the treasure chest onto Peter's hands and head. He slowly stood up. The chest moved a little unsteadily but remained on his head.

"Got it, Peter?" Wendy asked. Peter didn't say anything. He bent his knees and pushed off the ground hard. He floated up a few feet, the chest weighing him down.

"Got it," Peter strained. He went higher, his eyes locked on the chest above him. It swayed dangerously, but a screeching sound pulled Wendy and Tootles' attention away. Peter flew off. Tootles pulled Wendy behind the trees again. They hunkered down as a couple more ManyMores burst onto the trail. They looked in both directions and then followed after the queen. Tootles waited for them to get a few feet away before he jumped up, grabbed Wendy's arm, and sprinted down the trail. They made it a few hundred feet before being forced to hide behind the trees again. A shadow was growing larger and making its way toward them.

"Wendy? Tootles?"

"Peter? Is that you?" Wendy called out, standing up. She stepped out onto the trail and hugged Peter tightly. Tootles was a bit slower to step out of the hiding spot.

"You're back already?" Tootles asked. Peter pulled away from Wendy and shrugged.

"Once I got the chest balanced, it was fairly easy to get it to the boats," Peter replied.

"Well, that's good. Let's go then!" Wendy smiled. They were going to get to the lifeboat safely. She just knew it. She grabbed Peter's hand and started walking down the trail again. A rumbling sound started shaking the ground. Wendy looked behind her in horror. Peter and Tootles turned to see what she was looking at. Hundreds of Many-Mores were running in their direction. They had spread across the trail. From what Peter could tell, they were in a line throughout the forest too. There was nowhere to run but forward. He adjusted his grip on Wendy's hand and took off. Tootles was right behind them.

"We're never going to make it!" Wendy screamed. Peter ran faster. A few of the ManyMores attempted to run at them from a different angle, but Peter had pulled his sword out. He let go of Wendy's hand and sliced through them. He quickly caught back up with Wendy and Tootles.

"Keep going! We're almost there!" Peter roared as he sliced through another ManyMore. Wendy and Tootles were doing their best to keep going, but the ManyMores were starting to gain on them. They burst through the forest line and ran to the lifeboat. The treasure chest was sitting in the back, just like Peter said.

"Cast off!" Peter yelled. He swung his sword at a Many-More that had gotten too close. Wendy and Tootles pushed the lifeboat further into the water. The tide had come up a bit, which made it a bit easier.

"Get in," Tootles said as the boat was caught up in the water. Wendy climbed over the side without an argument. Tootles pushed the boat farther into the water. Wendy turned to watch Peter, as the ManyMore's all burst out of the forest at the same time. She covered her mouth with her hand, gasping.

"Tootles, look..." Wendy said, pointing. Tootles glanced behind him, not saying anything. He pushed the boat faster and farther into the ocean.

"Wait, what about Peter?" Wendy cried.

"He's fine. He can fly," Tootles responded. He hoisted himself over the edge of the boat and sat on the hard bench. He grabbed the oars and steered the boat. He started rowing quickly, trying to get the boat past the break.

"Peter!" Wendy cried. They were sitting beyond the breaking waves, watching as the ManyMores surrounded Peter. She could barely see him but knew he was still fighting. The flash of the sword told her that much.

"Come on, Peter!" Wendy cried. Suddenly, Peter shot straight up in the air, a few ManyMore's getting thrown in the process. He flew over to the lifeboat and crash-landed in the water. He surfaced and Tootles grabbed onto his collar, dragging him into the boat. Wendy grabbed her sword and poked at any mermaids who got too close to Peter. Tootles got Peter into the boat, dropping him on the floor. He took up his position and started rowing the boat as hard as he could. Wendy dropped to the ground, setting her sword aside. She caressed Peter's head, murmuring softly to him.

"We're here," Tootles panted. He swung the lifeboat to the side of the ship, grabbing the rope and tying them off. He climbed the ladder up to the deck. Wendy could hear him ordering the boys around. The twins poked their heads over the edge.

"Whoa! You really did get the treasure," One of them commented.

"Can you help me get it up there?" Wendy asked. The

twins glanced at each other and then slid down the ladder into the lifeboat.

"Sure!" They agreed at the same time. They turned to the chest and lifted it, causing the lifeboat to sway heavily. Nibs and Curly poked their heads over the edge.

"Hoard coming aboard!" One of the twins shouted. It caused a fit of laughter to go around, which delayed the retrieval of the chest. They heaved and pulled, finally getting the chest up onto the deck. Wendy glanced at the beach, noticing the ManyMores weren't pursuing them.

"They hate the water," Peter explained, his voice soft and weak. Wendy looked at him in concern.

"Don't speak, Peter. You need to save your strength," She said, patting his chest. He smiled at her. He raised a hand and caressed her cheek.

"I have strength enough for you," He responded. Wendy felt her cheeks warm. She cleared her throat and stood up. She gave the twins as much room as she could, watching as they carried Peter up onto the deck. She followed as the twins made their way up the ladder. As she made it onto the deck, she stopped and turned to the island. The ManyMores were starting to turn away. The queen was standing on the shore, staring in their direction. Wendy knew the queen couldn't actually see her, but she shivered nonetheless.

"That was certainly an adventure," Tootles said, coming to stand next to her. Wendy chuckled.

"You can say that again," She replied. Tootles gave her a smile and then went to stand at the helm. He gave orders to the boys who were milling around the deck, getting the ship underway. Wendy went to Peter's cabin and sat next to him while he rested. It took him a full day of rest, but by the next morning, he was back to his energetic self.

Wendy was standing at the edge of the ship, staring out

at the ocean. She had wrapped her arms around her body. Peter came to stand right behind her.

"So...still thinking about leaving?" Peter asked. She smiled, not bothering to turn around.

"I'd never dream of it. We still have a lot of adventures together," Wendy replied. Peter smiled, placing his hands on Wendy's shoulders. They stood like that while the ship cut through the water and took them onto the next adventure. They didn't know what to expect, but they were going to face it together.

THE END

THANKS FOR READING!

Don't forget to leave a review on Amazon. Reviews are extremely helpful for authors. Thank you for taking the time to support me and my work. I appreciate you!

DON'T FORGET TO SIGN UP FOR THE MONTHLY NEWSLETTER

To receive sneak peeks of my next work, giveaways, resources, bonus content, updates from me, info on new releases, and more:

WWW.KAYLEEWRITES.COM

ACKNOWLEDGMENTS

I'd like to acknowledge my husband, Russell. He made sure I had enough writing time to get this project done. He had no idea I was writing a story for him, but he was still incredibly supportive. I couldn't have done this without him. Thank you Russell for all that you do. I love you so much.

I also can't forget my friend - Jade. She has been so encouraging and supportive throughout my writing career. I honestly don't think I'd be anywhere near where I am today without her. She is always willing to listen and help me sort my brain out. Thank you Jade for everything!

ABOUT THE AUTHOR

Kaylee Johnston is an Urban Fantasy and Middle Grade author. She lives in Southern California with her husband and her beagle-basset hound, Ollie. When she's not writing, she's helping with her husband's business, reading, or snorkeling. If you bring an animal within her vicinity, all hope for productivity and focus is lost. She also doesn't know what else to put in this thing, so she's going to finish it here.